the
floor book

the
floor book

dominique coughlin

a comprehensive guide to
practical and decorative
floor treatments

Trafalgar Square Publishing

First published in the United States of America in 2002
by Trafalgar Square Publishing, North Pomfret, Vermont 05053

Printed in Italy

© Salamander Books Ltd., 2001
A member of the Chrysalis Group plc

ISBN I 57076 201 5

Library of Congress Catalog Card Number: 2001091505

All correspondence concerning the content of this volume should
be addressed to Salamander Books Ltd.

Editors: Helen Stone, Charlotte Davies, Stella Caldwell
Designers: John Heritage, Mark Holt
Reproduction: Studio Technology

CONTENTS

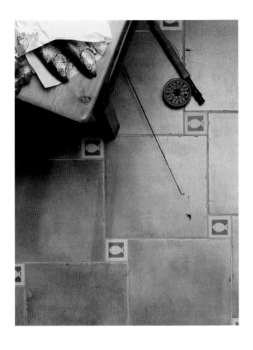

INTRODUCTION

WHAT COULD BE MORE IMPORTANT to the harmony of our home environment than the very ground we walk on? Flooring is a crucial element of interior design, affecting as it does our sense of balance and security. Our eye may be leading ahead and seeking the new, but the mind is always reckoning each step we must take to get there. It is impossible for flooring to be overlooked, but easy for it to be neglected. A reappraisal of our decorating priorities is long overdue. It's time to see floors as a fifth wall, a blank canvas to take the imprint of the best of creative decorating and design sensibilities.

It's essential to lay the right foundations. Floor covering is not a cover up, but an installation that should be undertaken with a thoroughness that will support passing traffic with confidence. And as far as floor cover goes, there have never been so many diverse possibilities. The right material for the right room is only half the story: design options continue to proliferate, adding to a history of architectural and design innovation that begins with ancients - stone, mosaics - and is now paving the way for the new millennium - glass perspex, paper.

Flooring unifies and defines a home, allowing you to seamlessly link rooms, or set them apart in terms of mood and function in a way that doesn't interfere with a building's proportions, yet subtly adjusts its sense of space. This book is a comprehensive guide to the options that await you, and includes ten practical step-by-step projects. You will find a wealth of materials at your feet, whether you are undertaking a quick update, or a painstaking restoration with a pot of paint.

LEFT: Hardwoods, such as oak, were commonly used for parquet flooring, providing a covering that improved, like fine wine, over the years. The mellow patina on this floor was achieved not by sanding and a coat of varnish, but by constant buffing and the tread of hundreds of feet.

BOARDS AND VENEERS

There can be no more effective way to achieve a stylish floor on a tight budget than to opt for bare floorboards. Not only does the colour of wood, with its honeyed hues, add a warmth to the tone of a room: wood is inherently warm underfoot, too. For these reasons, craftsman, for centuries, have created beautiful wooden floors. In every home, great planks sawn from the wide trunks of trees felled from ancient woodlands were polished and covered with simple rugs, while palaces were adorned with decorative parquets. Today we benefit from the insulating advantages of wooden floating floors, finished with decorative veneers and machine-cut patterning. Wooden floors have been painted and decorated over the centuries, too — often to mimic more expensive materials. In Scandinavia, floors were often adorned with strewn flowers, in imitation of the designs of fine needlepoint carpets, while more simple homes employed gay folk-art patterns of their own, such as using spattered paint, to brighten the appearance of worn, old floorboards.

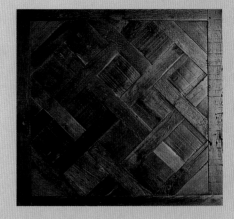

In the same way, today, a floor can become a canvas for the most elegant colour, for ingenious trompe l'oeil visual puns, or simply sanded and varnished for a straightforward, effective flooring treatment.

BARE BOARDS

Polished, oiled or varnished, wooden floorboards have a timeless, classic appeal and a utilitarian feel that makes them equally at home in a rustic setting, a stylish household or an ultra-modern apartment.

In an old house, what is discovered when old floor coverings are peeled back is often a revelation and an inspiration. In old timber-framed buildings, great elm or oak planks, as wide as the trunk of the tree from which they were sawn, can be found. Over the years, the wood will have lost moisture and shrunk, leaving raised knots and large gaps – but this is just part of their charm.

In the 18th century, interlocking tongue-and-groove pine floorboards were also a common flooring material and their close-fitting design made them perfect for blocking out draughts.

Old wood that has mellowed over the years brings a soft and warm ambience to a room and it is precisely this attribute that has made reclaimed woods so popular as flooring. Many elegant homes are now being created from barns and farm buildings, and even modern homes that seek a cosy, rustic look employ the worn beauty of old wood. The best method of fixing square-edged planks, whether on a concrete sub-floor or wooden joists, is to first lay a floating floor of tongue-and-groove chipboard. The planks can then be pinned and

LEFT: Natural floorboards are best suited to ground-floor rooms as they can be noisy to walk on. The honeyed tones of old wood suit a wide range of styles of decor and give a particularly warm welcome in an entrance hallway.

OPPOSITE LEFT: The parallel lines of floorboards give the illusion of lengthening a room in whichever direction they run, adding a much-needed sense of spaciousness to a small room and palatial qualities to larger ones.

OPPOSITE RIGHT: Once sealed with varnish, the warm, mellow tones of wooden floorboards can be enhanced by gently buffing with beeswax, which also gives added protection to the boards from scratching and scarring.

glued onto the chipboard with water-free adhesive, in the same way as parquet blocks are laid. This technique also offers a layer of insulation against draughts escaping from beneath the wood. Furthermore, as no new battening is employed, a hazardous 'trip' step is also avoided, although any exposed edges should always be chamfered down to the adjoining floor level.

Plain-edged boards are perhaps the most common discovery and, inevitably, in older houses, these could well be in need of some attention and restoration. Modern heating often causes moisture loss in floorboards, causing gaps to appear. A succession of carpets may

have been fitted over the years, and boards often need to be lifted for home improvements and maintenance, so it is common to find a dot-to-dot pattern of nail heads that may require countersinking or removing. Small gaps and holes can be easily filled with a flexible wood filler but, if the gaps are consistent, it will be easiest to lift the boards and re-lay them closer together, adding an extra board to make up the difference. Squeaking floorboards are a very common and irritating problem; the noise can sometimes be alleviated with the application of a little talcum powder or by screwing the offending plank to the joist so that it no longer moves with the pressure of footsteps.

WOODEN OVERLAY FLOORING

A fast pace of living has driven a slicker, glossier dimension into interior design. Narrow strip flooring has a sharp, sleek appeal. Sealed with tough lacquers, the wood gleams rather than basks in light and its finer proportions give pace to small-scale rooms. (Thin strips look too busy in large rooms.) Clean and smooth in appearance, wooden strip flooring adds elegance to modern interiors and is the staple specified by architects converting industrial space into apartments.

Laid on top of existing floorboards or a concrete floor, strip flooring is installed as an overlay floor. Thin, wooden, match-ended, tongue-and-groove strips are randomly laid; the tongue-and-groove board is slotted into the previous strip and invisibly nailed through the 'tongue' into the sub-floor beneath – either existing floorboards or marine ply screwed into concrete. For additional stability a water-resistant wood glue can also be used. Alternatively, the strip flooring can be laid onto existing joists or, in the case of a concrete floor, onto battens screwed to the concrete. Because each strip is match-ended, with a tongue-and-groove at each end as well as along its length, it is not necessary for the boards to be the exact length to fit the battens or joists, as they can support each other, and this feature significantly reduces trimming and wastage.

For a good, hard-wearing finish to a wooden overlay floor, it should be sealed with a couple of coats of acrylic lacquer. Thereafter, apart from regular dusting or wiping, it will benefit from a suitable dressing once or twice a year. As it is solid wood, if the floor becomes very worn it is possible to re-sand and seal it in order to restore it. However, there are limits to how many times this can be done before the tongue-and-groove joints at the centre of the strips weaken.

Decorative interest can be added to a wooden overlay floor with a border inset in contrasting wood, but the main floor is largely restricted to a simple, random strip design. The most common woods used for overlay floors are oak, which has a clean, warm colour, and maple, which is a richer, redder wood.

ABOVE: Sunlight refracts into softness, smoothing out the lines of a wooden floor that has been invisibly joined with tongue-and-groove edges – a technique that creates a strong and attractive floor with the minimum wastage of materials.

OPPOSITE: Pale pigments harmonize with white walls and furniture to create a clean, modern sanctuary. Sealed wooden floors can survive in a bathroom that is well ventilated, provided that it is used with care and thought.

SANDING FLOORBOARDS

Sanding existing floorboards is a simple way to transform a room and a professional finish is easy to achieve. Because of the dust created during the process, this is a job best done at the beginning of renovation projects. If you are doing a room in isolation, seal it off from the rest of the house and keep it ventilated. Drum sanding machines can be hired from DIY shops, and the sandpaper is usually provided on a sale-or-return basis. Wear an efficient dust mask and, as the machines can be noisy, wear ear plugs also.

1 To prepare the floorboards for sanding, use a nail punch and hammer to tap down any protruding nails until the heads are below the surface of the boards. A claw hammer can be used to lift out any proud nails. It is important to do this properly; nails are likely to rip the sanding paper. Carefully read the safety instructions supplied with your drum sander. The cable should be kept over your shoulder, leading away from you. It is best to start in the centre of the room working outwards. Begin the sanding process using the coarsest sheet of sandpaper.

2 Tilt the drum sander back slightly, switch on and slowly lower to the floor. Work diagonally guiding the machine across the floor to smooth down ridges on the board edges. Switch off when one length of the floor is complete, turn the machine and continue. If the sandpaper rips the noise can be alarming; however you just need to switch off the machine, and unplug it while you change the sandpaper disc. Empty the dust bag of the first collection of dirty sawdust. When the whole floor has been sanded repeat with medium discs of sandpaper.

3 The clean sawdust from the second sanding can now be used to fill fine gaps in the floor. Mix the sawdust into a paste with PVA glue and smooth mixture into gaps with a filling knife. Allow to dry. Give the floor a final sanding with the fine discs of sandpaper. Finish the unsanded edges of the room with an edging sander, again working through the three grades of sandpaper, from coarse to fine. Finally seal the floor with two coats of acrylic varnish. Make sure the surface is dust-free and use a good quality brush. Allow the floor to dry thoroughly between coats.

PARQUET FLOORING

The crown prince of wooden flooring is undoubtedly the parquet floor. It was, and still is today, the most expensive form of wooden flooring, in which beautiful woods are used to form an intricate pattern that plays on the subtlety of the wood grain to create a superbly crafted floor. Experienced craftsmen have an eye for the precise laying of each piece of wood in relation to the play of light in a room to create a calm, smooth expanse of flooring where the eye can detect no awkward cuts or negotiations of room shape, though many may have had to be considered during the laying process.

The earliest parquet floors date back as far as the middle ages,

with an example of a simple parquet floor existing in a 13th century church. Parquet became most fashionable in French houses in the 17th century and in the grand houses of Russia – both countries that had good sources of timber. The parquet floor reached its zenith in the French chateaux that were built in the 18th century, and many parquet patterns today take their names from these fine houses: for example, the latticework design of Chantilly or the mitred pattern of D'Arambert. The elegance and beauty of these floors, which have withstood centuries of wear with grace and fortitude, is timeless.

Parquet floors started to become more commonplace in the

late Victorian home, and are a characteristic feature of Edwardian and earlier 20th-century buildings. The beauty of its geometry lent itself to this crossroads point in decoration, where the modernist Art Deco style and the fine craftsmanship of the Arts and Crafts movement sought expression. From the 1920s, parquet flooring came to be a feature of all civic buildings, from the smart city buildings of the world's growing metropolises to provincial church halls, meeting houses and school halls. The parquet floor also embodies a mood of glamour, evoking the ambience of old dance halls and coffee houses.

Parquet is not restricted to period-style homes: it looks equally good in minimal, contemporary interiors where texture rather than pattern sets the rhythm of a room. Chocolate-brown woods are a signature choice in glamorous habitats for urban living where open-plan designs require a good-looking but multi-functional floor. In situations where flooring has to run smoothly through spaces that serve for both work and play, parquet is a particularly good choice.

OPPOSITE: Illustrating superbly the intricate play of light and shade that is created by the precise use of differently coloured woods, this fine floor creates an almost three-dimensional effect where mitred diagonals cross the main woven pattern.

ABOVE: Though created from vast quantities of separate wood blocks, parquet flooring is so precisely fitted and finished that the result is a sheer, gleaming expanse of polished flooring that fits equally into traditional and modern settings.

RIGHT: Blonde woods have been used here to create a pale, light-reflecting parquet floor that gives a fresh, contemporary look. The tongue and groove planks are extremely hard-wearing and can tolerate high foot traffic.

TRADITIONAL PARQUET DESIGNS

Parquet floors survive well and are still to be found intact in period homes. Most were not removed when wooden floors fell from favour in the 1960s, but covered instead with carpet.

Fine hardwoods were the first choice for decorative parquet floors. Lustrous dark floors were created from such exotic species as panga panga and teak, while the mood of the jazz age was expressed with blonde woods such as ash, whose creamy white grain brought light flooding into Art Deco buildings. Other traditional hardwoods, such as oak, with its wide grain and light nutty hues, maple and the more affordable chestnut were also commonly used.

Many of these woods are available today from reclaimed sources, while sustainable hardwoods, such as oak, now benefit from slow kiln-drying, which gives them a richness and seasoning. It is also possible to buy parquet floors that have been salvaged from old schools or halls and which can then be re-laid. Older woods, of course, have the benefit of bearing the history of their previous life, with scars and marks adding to their beauty and character.

Parquet floors are laid with square-edged wooden blocks rather than with tongue-and-groove strips. They used to be fixed with hot bitumen, and you may still find remnants of the black adhesive on par-

LEFT: Hardwoods, such as oak, were commonly used for parquet flooring, providing a covering that improved, like fine wine, over the years. The mellow patina on this floor was achieved not by sanding and a coat of varnish, but by constant buffing and the tread of hundreds of feet.

RIGHT: A variety of warm-toned hardwoods has been used to create the geometric designs on this floor, which is alive with the movement of light and shade achieved by its intricate assembly of cross and diagonal patterning.

quet floors bought from salvage yards: this can be chipped or sanded off before re-laying. If pieces of parquet have worked loose, they can be replaced, using a water-free flooring adhesive spread.

Because parquet is made of solid wood – unlike today's modern veneers or thin tongue-and-groove boards – neglected floors can be brought back to life by sanding, finishing with a suitable, quick-drying, satin finish seal. This is not really a job that should be tackled by the amateur, however. Instead, make the most of original parquet by entrusting its restoration to a professional. Any extra cost will be well repaid by the quality of the restoration work achieved.

Part of the art of laying parquet is in the finishing. A mas-

ter craftsman will, for example, painstakingly countersink any tiny wood pins and fill any small gaps between the wood blocks with a hand-worked putty that includes linseed oil and natural pigments in its mixture. Keeping the putty to a workable consistancy and creating just the right match to the wood tone takes a skilled eye, but the finished results will be seamless. The traditional beeswax finish is also a labour-intensive indulgence, something that belongs in the grand houses of the past with their armies of below-stairs servants.

A prized parquet floor makes a good case for the reintroduction of 'indoor' shoes, as stiletto heels and steel caps will seriously undermine all the work involved in keeping the floor looking good.

CREATING PARQUET FLOORING

Like the fine marquetry of inlaid furniture, parquet flooring is the most sophisticated choice of wooden flooring because of the precision required in its creation. There are a number of classic parquet patterns that are commonly found: one of the favourites is herringbone, with its handsome chevrons giving a direction to the wood. Other popular patterns are brick, ladder and basketweave designs. Typically, the English style of laying parquet is with the pattern square to the wall, contained within a border, whereas the French style is to have the pattern diagonal to the wall and bleeding off.

More elaborate parquet floors employ geometry to develop these patterns. Patterns are contained in a field – a panel of parquet that is framed by mitred 'cuts' that interlock and form a larger inter-locking pattern. Skilled craftsman can develop this geometry further, creating circles and other stunning patterns, which are infilled with basic patterns to create a visually stunning whole. In some countries, such as Italy, the similarity between the parquet floor and marquetry is emphasized with elaborate borders containing florid patterns constructed in boldly contrasting woods – a fashion that is now aided by sophisticated machine-cutting technology.

For the traditional craftsman, however, most of the work and skill of laying parquet goes into planning and measuring. Parquet flooring today is laid onto a sub-floor. In the case of an existing concrete floor, this should first have flooring-grade chipboard cut in and laid as a floating floor, with a thin polystyrene underlay for insulation.

LEFT: The rhythm of the parquet flooring pattern can be subtly altered by introducing coloured 'accent' woods into the overall design, thereby creating a bright contemporary look with this traditional flooring medium.

OPPOSITE LEFT: A modern monochrome room need not be jarred by the brown-to-honey palette of a wooden floor. Here, a pale white stained finish on a modern parquet floor harmonizes the mood into the overall scheme.

OPPOSITE RIGHT: This classic parquet floor demonstrates its versatility in a home setting, moving easily across the Deco-inspired interior scheme, from the living room into a dining room-cum-conservatory area.

Existing joists can be covered with chipboard screwed to the boards, while an existing softwood floor is covered with 6mm ($^1\!/4$in) plywood nailed to the floorboards. The parquet is then laid using a water-free adhesive, while the fine joints between the square-edged blocks can be grouted with a mixture of filler and clean dust from a first sanding. The floor is then sanded and screened before sealing.

The look of a parquet floor can be achieved with ready-manufactured boards, which are easy to install and more affordable than the real thing. Parquet designs are mounted onto tongue-and-groove boards, which are then slotted together and laid as an overlay. The machine-cut parquet designs give a precisely designed look, and the boards can be laid either so that the pattern bleeds off the edges of the room, or is contained within a border.

Although lacking the character and longevity of the real thing, parquet-finished boards are an easy and affordable way of bringing texture and subtle patterning to a floor.

WOOD VENEER FLOORING

Pattern and colour really come into play with the use of wood veneers. While overlay wooden flooring is generally limited to only a few options, wood veneers open up a much greater range of design and colour possibilities, from the youthful blush of cherrywood to the rich grains of mahogany.

The wood veneer is cut into small strips, like a slice cut from the top of a wooden parquet block. The strip is then adhered to a strong base, usually of high density fibreboard, with an added layer of insulation. The veneer strips are then bonded together to form 'staves' or boards. Precision-made by machines, the staves can be simply slotted together. This is known as a 'floating' floor, a type of flooring that is very advantageous for homes that are being refurbished, as it can be

laid on top of existing flooring without excessively raising the height of the floor: generally only 1.5cm ($\frac{5}{8}$in) is gained, which should cause a minimum of problems with existing doors and adjoining floors.

Compared to exposed floorboards, a floating hardwood floor offers greater comfort, as there are no unwanted gaps for draughts to whistle through. Dirt and dust can also blow through such gaps, so a sealed floor offers a cleaner, less dusty environment. Most suppliers of floating floors recommend that a damp-proof sheet is put down before the boards are laid; a further sheet of insulation material, either of rubber or cork, can also be laid. As well as minimizing draughts and dust, this has the added advantage of ensuring that a floating floor is far less noisy than ordinary floorboards or, indeed, solid parquet floors. The finished effect is sleek and glamorous and is ideal for making a statement in hallways or formal living rooms.

Floating floors are relatively easy to install though, as with all floor treatments, professional fitting is recommended. The panels are laid, butting neatly against each other with an expansion gap left around the edge of the room and around any holes cut for pipes; these gaps can be covered by a matching skirting or moulded beading. As wood is continuously expanding and contracting with changes in temperature and humidity, this gap allows for the staves to swell and shrink without disturbing the floor.

Although wood veneers have the advantage of being more versatile and cosy than conventional floorboards, they are not as hardy or forgiving as their solid counterparts. As in veneered furniture, the thin wooden layer is a delicate medium that can only withstand light re-sanding and sealing. This type of flooring is designed to stand up to normal wear and tear, but care should be taken to avoid excessively punishing treatment, as unsightly chips and scratches can occur, and these are difficult to eradicate. Excessive exposure to water can also pose a threat, lifting the veneer and causing warping. Such floors are, therefore, not recommended for use in bathrooms.

OPPOSITE: A wood veneer floor is a functional and good-looking choice in a kitchen area, with a finish that is easily wipeable yet warm and welcoming underfoot. It fits into this bright, modern kitchen with effortless charm.

RIGHT: A hardwearing option, with their tough laquered finish, veneered floors have the natural appeal of a solid wooden floor yet are well able to withstand the wear and tear of heavy traffic areas in a busy family household.

BELOW: When used as a veneer, unusual and richly coloured woods can be used in a more cost-effective and affordable way. Here, a cherry veneer fills this light-filled apartment with a warmth that belies the lack of soft furnishings.

FAUX WOODEN FLOORING

Professionals agree that it is inadvisable to use wooden flooring in a kitchen or bathroom, where excessive splashing and the severe drying caused by modern central-heating systems can cause the wood to warp and split. Of course these considerations can be countered with thoughtful attention but, in busy households, the problem can be solved by laying a laminated wood-effect floor that gives the sleek appearance of a strip or parquet wooden floor but has the durability, wearability and even washability of vinyl floor coverings.

Laminated faux wooden flooring was developed in the 1970s and is now a widely available and acceptable alternative to wood strip flooring. The technique is fascinatingly obvious. A photograph of a real wooden floor is mounted onto a base board – usually a high-density fibreboard made from bonded wood waste, which is an

OPPOSITE ABOVE: A facsimile of randomly laid, rich, walnut, wood-strip flooring brings a cosy, cabin warmth to this bedroom. In low traffic rooms such as this, wood laminate flooring is exceptionally easy to maintain.

OPPOSITE BELOW: The skills of a master carpenter have been effortlessly reproduced in this dining-room floor. Small diamond motifs, precisely inset into the richly coloured wooden strips, lend a sense of occasion.

BELOW: Faux wooden flooring can imitate the most complex and expensive wood flooring designs. Here diagonally cut wood strips, laid in an intricate diamond pattern, have been reproduced.

extremely stable medium and one that is resistant to warping. The photograph is coated with a tough laminated surface of polyvinyl chloride (PVC) or a form of resin that is impervious to water yet gives a finish resembling the lacquered sheen of strip flooring.

Wood laminate flooring is usually laid in exactly the same way as a wooden floating floor and thus may not need professional installation. If the laminate is made from a tough resin, the flooring will have impressive resistance to burns and scratches and is easy to maintain as it can be simply wiped clean. In contrast, faux wooden vinyl flooring requires maintenance using dedicated dressing products.

Its resilient, wipeable surface makes laminate flooring ideal for kitchens and, because it features photographic imagery, any type of grain, effect, colour or pattern can be achieved, such as imitation parquet or finely cut marquetry patterns, both materials traditionally considered too fine for the ravages of kitchen life. As a laminate, delicate patterns can be reproduced and sealed beneath a protective layer, elevating the workrooms of a home into elegant living spaces.

INTRODUCING COLOUR

Inferior woods have been coloured, grained and stained for centuries. In less affluent homes, humble softwoods were enriched with simple stains made from vegetable dyes, even tea, which were used to produce water-based colours for creating imitation oaks and hardwoods.

With today's influence leaning toward bare boards, there is a wide variety of proprietary wood stains available. After sanding, stripped wood can look brash and new and wood stains are ideal for adding an antique patina or for transforming floorboards into an imitation of more expensive wooden planks. The beauty of stains lies in their translucency, which allows for all the knots, grains and subtle shading of the wood to shine through while still allowing the colour to penetrate the surface of the wood. For an even finish, small gaps in the wood can be filled with dust collected from the second sanding of the floor, mixed with a cellulose-based adhesive. (Dust from the first sanding should not be used as this is often sullied with dirt and old dressings.) Once the gaps are filled, a final fine sanding leaves the boards well prepared for staining.

A wide range of colours is available and these are often displayed on wood samples at specialist paint stores; many stores will also demonstrate colours mixed to order before a quantity is bought. Absorbency varies from wood to wood, so a sample test should be carried out in an unobtrusive area, painting a small patch and leaving it to dry thoroughly to see how the colour develops.

Oil-based stains, which can be thinned with white spirit, are popular as they add a deeper colour to floorboards. The stain can be applied with a rag, working on two or three boards at a time, and always working in the direction of the grain and, of course, towards the door. Masked or stencilled designs using several colours can also be created in stains, although the floor should first be prepared with a coat of shellac to prevent the colours from bleeding together. A stained floor should finally be sealed with an oil-based varnish, which will add depth and give a tough hard-wearing finish.

ABOVE: A traditional coat of hard-wearing oil-based floor varnish brings a warmth and gloss to newly sanded floorboards while still allowing their fresh smoothness to convey a uniquely clean, contemporary mood.

OPPOSITE: Different wood stains are produced to imitate various wood types and these can be used in conjunction with each other to create novel designs and patterns, such as this over-blown modern interpretation of faux parquet.

COLOUR-STAINED BOARDS

A wider palette of wood stains becomes available with the use of acrylic water-based colours. These colours are mainly intended for use on furniture, as the water content can raise the grain of wooden floorboards. However, they can be appropriate as a way of integrating your floor 'canvas' into the room without blocking it with solid colour.

For this purpose, you can also quite simply choose any colour that is available as a water-based matt emulsion paint and double its content with water to create a satisfactory wood stain. Any colour option for a stain becomes a possibility by mixing colours yourself, including lightening with white or enriching with reds and blues. The resulting semi-opaque colour gives a finish that can cleverly show off the natural grain of wood while disguising any unwanted rawness, and for this purpose, diluted water-based matt paint is ideal.

A classic look for introducing colour on a floor is to create the

LEFT: Pale, lime-washed floorboards are characteristic of the cool, elegant Scandanavian interiors that are still very much admired and emulated today. Blue and grey-green pigments here add a more muted tone.

RIGHT: Wood stains can be built up to create rich, deep colours – such as the vibrant blue in this charming study – while still allowing the natural grain and textures of the wood to shine through as an intrinsic part of the interior.

effect of limed oak wood. Lime-wash has been applied to wood since medieval times, primarily to make it unpalatable to parasites. The effect, however, leaves an attractive silvery patina that is once again a fashionable effect. It is easy to work diluted white paint into floor-boards to achieve the same effect: this 'wood wash' can be applied with a sponge-head mop, but thought and care should be given to applying the wash evenly so that the final effect is not patchy. For a more muted look, diluted blue-greens and greys also work well.

Lightly stained wooden floorboards make a good, primed background for the introduction of pattern. Naturalistic designs or solid blocks of colour can be added to the sheer canvas, while a light overlay of stencilling can further enhance the look. A wooden floor stained with a complementary yet softer tone of a woven rug or other furnishing accessory accent colour is another good way to complete the look of a room. The finished result will be gently harmonious and lived-in, yet with a practical feel too.

For pale wood wash effects, it is best to use an acrylic water-based varnish, which will not add any colour to the floor, but remain clear. Easy to apply and use, the varnish should, however, go on only when the wood wash has been allowed to dry thoroughly, in case the water content picks up the colour of the wash, moving it around with the varnish and thus making the finished effect patchy and uneven.

FAUX LIMED FLOORS

Limed floors are increasingly popular, producing a lighter, more modern feel on wooden floorboards. The effect is achieved by rubbing limed paste or wax onto the floor, rubbing it down and then sealing with two or more coats of lacquer. Liming was traditionally done on oak; the effect is less pronounced on soft woods, such as pine. A similar effect to liming can be rather more easily achieved by working a diluted white paint solution into clean, bare floorboards. Diluted greys and blue-green colours can also be used for a more muted effect.

1 Whether you intend to lime a floor in the traditional way, by working liming wax into the surface, or go for the easier option of applying a lime-effect wood wash, it is imperative that you start with perfectly clean, dust- and grease-free floorboards. If the floor is an old one, ensure that any previous finishes are completely removed, by sanding if necessary. Remove any grease marks with white spirit. If the floor is of hardwood, then you might like to open up the grain first by rubbing with wire wool, or roughing up the surface with a bronze-bristled hand brush.

2 Finish cleaning the floor by brushing up any dust or debris. A 'tack cloth', which is obtainable from good DIY retailers, is very effective at picking up any surface dust that would mar the final effect once lacquer has been applied. Mix up a solution of water and matt emulsion paint in your chosen colour. White gives the closest imitation of a traditional limed floor, but you can use any colour. Test on an unobtrusive area that the solution is to your liking, adjusting if necessary. Using an 8–9cm brush, start applying the paint in the corner furthest from the door.

3 Continue applying the diluted paint solution to the floor, trying to ensure that the coverage is even and that you don't go over the same area twice. For speed, the solution can be applied with a sponge-headed mop, but this makes even application more difficult to achieve. Once you have covered the entire floor, leave it until it is completely dry – this may take 24 hours, depending on conditions. Finally seal the floor with two coats of acrylic, water-based varnish, lightly sanding the first coat when it is completely dry, before applying the final coat.

PAINTED WOOD FLOORS

There is no quicker way to ring the changes in a room than by applying a coat of paint. Paint works wonders on the most tired plaster or woodwork, bringing a breath of fresh air – and the same is true for floors. Bare boards can provide attractive flooring, but often the removal of existing coverings is disappointing. In many cases, second-rate wood is used for floorboards in homes where carpet or coverings were intended, so it can be a waste of energy and time to sand, seal and polish knotty, pitted and nail-scarred timber. Instead, it may be more fun to let such a floor benefit from a dense layer of colour.

A single expanse of colour will instantly smarten the tattiest wooden floor, while a soft off-white will make a room look bigger, visually pushing back the walls and setting a cool, calm, modernist tone. Soft blues and greys also set a restful mood, while a classic Wedgwood-blue looks elegant with creamy white walls and is a good

ABOVE: Floorboards painted in a milky white brighten this small bathroom and contrast with the sunny yellow walls. The pale colour lifts the floor and balances the tall windows of the room. A bright rug provides comfort underfoot.

LEFT: Strong, bright colours have a bold visual impact and are especially suitable for children's rooms where they can be used in full force to evoke a specific theme or mood. Pink-painted floorboards add here to the kaleidoscopic charm.

OPPOSITE: Dark painted floorboards in this grand, white-painted music room lend a sense of depth and majesty, pushing the floor further down from the panelled walls and emphasizing their graceful proportions.

foundation for disparate styles of furniture and furnishings.

Left bare, a painted floor seems to demand a minimalist approach to furniture and furnishings, suiting simple pieces that sit gracefully in the clean space. However, a painted floor can also act as a subdued backdrop when partnered with cleverly contrasting woven rugs, floor canvases or tapestry carpets.

The preparation and painting of a wooden floor is a relatively straightforward process. The boards need to be scrubbed with a stiff brush and soapy water, with excess water mopped up quickly with a sponge. Where there are persistent greasy or sticky patches, a little white spirit on a rag should be used to clean them off to ensure even absorption of the paint. The floor should then be left to dry thoroughly before further preparation with a coat of acrylic primer.

There are several types of paint suitable for use on the floor and the manufacturer's instructions should be followed carefully to ensure correct application. Oil-based eggshell paints give good wear on floorboards and, with custom mixing services available, the spectrum of colours is vast. However, a normal matt emulsion paint serves just as well and can be applied easily with a roller before sealing with two thin coats of a clear, acrylic floor varnish.

ADDING STRIPES AND CHECKS

Incorporating pattern into a painted floor can be stunningly effective, even when the pattern consists of nothing more complicated than simple stripes and checks. Stripes have an understated chic and can actually help to balance the proportions of a room. For example, painted widthwise in a long narrow room, stripes give an enhanced impression of breadth. It is often suggested that the width of the floorboard should be used as a grid for measuring out patterns but, for a more balanced effect, this should be waived in favour of proportions that complement and enhance the shape of the particular room.

While there is always room for the jazzy, the psychedelic and the kitsch, stripes on floors are best painted in tones that are close in shade. Strongly contrasting shades are fine for walls but they can be downright hazardous for floors, as the eye can easily misinterpret them as steps. For bold contrast, a classic chequerboard pattern in stark black and white always looks impressive. Equally, the same design in softer, muted shades gives a traditional Scandinavian feel.

Checks are easy to create, with the lighter base colour applied first in matt emulsion or eggshell paint. Stripes are marked using a long ruler and masked with low-tack tape, leaving the in-between spaces to be filled with the contrasting colour.

It is a highly skilled job to lay tiles in a diagonal pattern, but easy to imitate this effect in paint. The floor is dissected by drawing lines across the floor from the centres of opposite walls: the point where the two lines cross marks the room's centre. A square template is cut to the required size and placed in the centre of the floor, corners aligned with the pencil lines. The first tile is marked here and repeat tiles are drawn along the pencil line, 'cutting' the tile when it reaches the wall. The outer edges of each alternate row of squares are masked with tape before filling in with the contrasting colour.

More complex patterns can be created by building on this basic technique. The introduction of a border, for example, gives a trompe l'oeil carpet effect. Whatever the design – and sometimes the simplest are the smartest – a patterned floor has the advantage over plain painted floorboards as it shows less wear.

OPPOSITE: For the simplest chequerboard design, low-tack tape can be centred along the marked lines of a chequerboard pattern and painted over to leave a natural wood border in imitation of an inlaid pattern, as shown here.

ABOVE LEFT: Drawn to scale on graph paper, patterns taken from textiles – such as the geometric symbols woven into kelims – can be easily mapped out. For a neat finish, the repeat pattern is contained within a border.

LEFT: A chic tile effect is created through the imaginative use of just two colours that are sympathetic in tone to the natural wood floor plus the simple use of keystones, which are marked at the corner of each painted tile.

PAINTING A CHEQUERED FLOOR

For floorboards that are badly pitted or scarred, a chequerboard design offers an elegant alternative to plain painted boards. This versatile design can be created in any colour combination, selecting the size of the panels to suit the proportions of the room. By using the width of the floorboards as a standard measure, you can dispense with the necessity of laboriously measuring across the breadth of the floor to mark the pattern. Instead, simply use this measurement to mark the checks along the length of each board.

1 Prepare the floor by sanding the boards and removing any dust, dirt and grease with white spirit. Allow the wood to dry thoroughly before applying two coats of off-white eggshell paint, sanding the floor between coats. When the second coat is dry, mask off the inside edges of every third board with low-tack masking tape. Using a ruler and pencil, mark the same pattern down the length of the floor, applying masking tape in the same fashion to complete the pattern.

2 Pinch small chunks from the edges and surface of an ordinary synthetic household sponge: this will ensure a painted surface that is irregularly pitted. Dip the sponge into mid-blue eggshell paint and scrape off the excess. Dab the paint into the larger exposed squares, ensuring that the paint is applied right up to the edges of the masking tape but not beyond. The painted surface should be lightly mottled, while still evenly covering the exposed area.

3 Wash the paint out of the sponge and leave it to dry. Dip the sponge into navy-blue eggshell paint, remove the excess and apply to the small squares, creating the same mottled effect as before. When the paint is touch-dry, carefully peel off the masking tape to reveal the chequerboard pattern. Allow the paint to dry thoroughly before sealing the floor with two coats of clear acrylic or polyurethane varnish, lightly sanding the surface between coats for a smooth finish.

STENCILS AND STAMPS

At a time when there is a burgeoning development in computer-aided design and it seems only a matter of time before we can select a virtual interior in which to spend the evening, a passionate revival of the simplest and most primitive pattern-printing effects is sharing the limelight. Stencilling and stamping are strangely similar yet opposite techniques and seem to be as old as time itself; we remember stencils from schooldays as cards with cut-out shapes for making flowers or letters; similarly, stamping has its place in our earliest recollections of

artistic endeavour – a potato cut in half and chiselled to form a triangle or star, which was then dipped in paint and printed on paper.

These same techniques have been used for centuries to adorn interiors, and examples of early stencilling have been found alongside decorative painting as far back as the middle ages. Stencilling and stamping are useful techniques for decorating large areas such as floors as the print is light and allows the background to remain an intrinsic part of the design. For this reason they are particularly compatible with wooden floors, and motifs can be easily applied while still allowing the natural grain of the floor to show through.

A great and varied choice of manufactured stencils and stamps is widely available, but it is almost as easy to trace designs from books or other decorative sources to create original designs cut from manila card for stencils or from fine foam sponges to make stamps.

These treatments require some preparatory work: floorboards need to be sanded and a background stain or colour wash applied. Before mapping out repeat, all-over patterns, mark the centre of the floor by drawing a line from the centre points of opposite walls to find the central intersection. Repeat spacing can then be worked out from this point. Alternatively, a stencil or stamped motif, such as simple stars or sprigs of flowers, can be applied at random, creating an organically balanced effect by eye. The design is not limited to all-over designs as this technique is ideal for creating decorative borders or for making more impressive statements, such as printing a noble motto onto a painted doormat or a central rose. Best results are achieved by using the proper equipment: stencils, for example, are best applied with a stencil brush. Both techniques should be practised on paper first to prevent over- or under-loading of the brush or stamp. Specialist paints are widely available for use with these techniques, though matt emulsion can also be used. Avoid eggshell or oil-based paints as they are too thick for printing detail. When dry, the floor should be finished with two or three coats of acrylic floor varnish.

ABOVE: A welcoming symbol of formal berry wreaths stencilled across the limed wooden floorboards creates a Scandinavian mood in this living room, a theme that is further evoked by the simple checked curtains.

LEFT: A Moorish influence creates a noble, ancient atmosphere in this bathroom. The Gothic arch is echoed with a fairy-tale stylized motif printed across the wooden floor and around the roughly plastered walls.

OPPOSITE: Elaborate patterns can be built up using a succession of stamps or stencils of sympathetic shapes and styles. Repeat border designs are particular effective, as are inset panels with a central rose.

41

STENCILLING A BORDER

One of the most effective ways of adding decoration to a wooden floor is to use stencils to create repeat motifs. All-over patterns can be painted in this way, although it is a time-consuming process and can make a floor look cluttered. However, the same technique can be used very effectively to paint a simple border featuring a single motif; two tones of the same colour paint are used here to give the design added depth. This look has an understated elegance that works well whatever the size of the room.

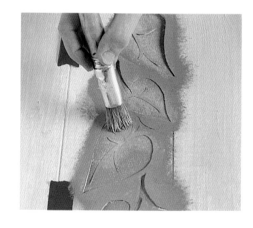

1 Beginning with sanded boards, remove any excess dirt, dust and grease with white spirit. Apply two coats of off-white eggshell paint, allowing the paint to dry and lightly sanding the floor between each coat. Dip the tip of a dry 10cm (4in) decorator's brush into beige eggshell paint and scrap off any excess. Holding the brush at a 45° angle, drag it along the floor surface in the direction of the grain to create a streaked effect. Allow to dry.

2 Draw simple leaf shapes onto a sheet of stencil card to create a border motif. Cut out the shape with a craft knife. Lightly mark the position of the border on the floor, keeping it equidistant from and parallel to the walls. Starting in one corner, lay the stencil on the floor, holding it in place with masking tape. Dip the end of a stencilling brush into mid-green emulsion paint, remove any excess, and apply the paint through the stencil.

3 Keeping the stencil in place, dip the tip of a second stencilling brush into pale green emulsion paint and gently stipple over part of the leaf design to create a soft, mottled effect. Carefully lift the stencil, move it along and reposition it next to the first motif. Apply paint in the same way, continuing the process until the border is complete. Allow the paint to dry thoroughly before sealing the floor with two coats of matt polyurethane varnish.

FLAGSTONES AND TILES

The solidity of a hard-surfaced floor seems to root a home in time. Tiled, stone and ceramic floors have, over the centuries, paved the floors of palaces, temples and churches with grave majesty and jubilant ostentation. In more humble homes, they served as the only barrier against the cold earth beneath, at the same time retaining the heat from the fire and repelling the danger of wayward cinders.

Glazed ceramic tiles have long been favoured as a cool, hygienic floor surface – but not just for kitchens and bathrooms: they are commonly used to introduce decorative flooring elements around fireplaces, porches and hallways.

Quarry tiles are particularly popular as a hard flooring material, and come in a range of shapes, colours and surface textures. Terracotta tiles are similar though, being porous, require sealing. Prices depend on whether the tiles are machine-made or, more expensively, hand-made.

After more than a century of rapid industrial and technological advancement, a more natural, sensual aesthetic is now coming into ascendancy, and stone floors, with their inherent beauty and longevity, are once more finding their way back into the heart of interiors.

TRADITIONAL FLAGS

Riven or honed flags of slate or stone have been used as flooring for centuries. After the 1900s, tastes changed as new materials, from linoleum to easily affordable carpet, superannuated the slow, costly business of quarrying. There remains an inviting and honest appeal in flagstones, however: equally at home in a simple rustic cottage or in a functional architectural space, their purity has much to offer.

Originally, the choice of stone used for paving was limited by the sheer effort of transportation to local resources. Thus old build-

ings and their interiors maintained a harmony with the landscape in which they were built, and we still associate regions with certain colouring: rich reds, golden sand colours, pale limes or inky blues. Today, however, it is possible to choose from a wider palette made up of flags that are quarried around the world. Slates and stones can now be transported from India and China, offering a wonderfully rich spectrum to the designer – similar to that of the gemologist, but at a much lower price. Flagstones can now compare in price to wool carpet, yet they have the potential to last more than a lifetime.

At the same time as newly quarried materials from around the world have become available, an enormous increase in salvaged building materials has also occurred. It is now possible to buy flagstones that are thousands of years old, intact and enriched with the patina of time, brought back from ancient buildings in Europe and the Middle East. Because old flagstones would have been hand-cut to a much greater thickness than that of today's machine-cut stones, salvaged flags with a romantic provenance can be cut across to make a 'second-face' flagstone. Although such a stone will not have the worn patina that results from centuries of footfall, it is still a rare and interesting flooring material, which can be sold at a lesser price.

Practical factors have also helped to make flagstones a viable flooring choice. Rapid advancements in heating technology, such as maintenance-free polypropylene pipes, now mean that underfloor heating is widely installed in newly built homes. Flagstones retain ambient temperature, so whereas before they were known to stay as cold as the earth below, now they can contribute to heating conservation by retaining the heat from under-floor pipes.

Advances in machine-cutting technology has resulted in flagstones that are much thinner and lighter than traditional flags. This makes them easy to lay, even in upstairs bathrooms, as long as a strong plywood sub-floor has been installed to prevent any movement that may cause the grout between the stones to break up.

ABOVE: The riven texture of traditionally quarried flagstones gives this room a cherished mellowness and warmth that belies its rock-solid foundations, at the same time evoking the stability and enduring qualities of a bygone age.

LEFT: Keystone insets add a simple decorative note to a classic flagstone passageway. Colour variations in the flags, together with light reflections in their gleaming patina, add to the warmth and character of the area.

OPPOSITE: Pale-coloured, offset flagstones create a cool, airy entrance hallway, which serves well to withstand the daily incursion of mud-encrusted footwear in a busy country household, while still retaining a measure of elegance.

SLATE FLAGS

A sedimentary rock formed by the action of water washing against mud, slate has a part crystalline sheen that enriches its dark composition. Like sandstone, its riven surface gives a textured plane when used as a flooring material.

Slate has a very low porosity (of only one or two per cent) and, in the 19th century, it came to replace other stones as a flooring material due to its ability to prevent damp penetrating floors. For this reason, also, it is found in the cellars of buildings; today, this gives slate a historical design context in basement rooms and apartments.

The rich, dark hues of slate give it a rugged appeal, in keeping with a rustic aesthetic for cottage or farmhouse interiors or, equally, for a sombre, antique setting for a Gothic-inspired room. Since slate will not react to domestic acids, it makes a hard-working kitchen floor, which, when sealed, will become quite impervious to water. In a modern context, slate flags can create a stylishly sleek, architectural kitchen when teamed with polished slate work surfaces. Slate was also one of the traditional surfaces for the patissier, so any cook with a passion for pastrymaking will benefit from its cool temperature.

LEFT: The green and coppery variegation on the slate flags in this modern kitchen indicate their eastern provenance. The importation of slate from India and China has significantly increased the range of colours now currently available.

OPPOSITE LEFT: Modern slate tiles are more thinly cut than traditional flags, making them a functional option for upstairs rooms, such as this bathroom. The low-porosity of slate makes it an ideal flooring material in potentially wet areas.

OPPOSITE RIGHT: Quarried slate flags served traditionally as durable, damp-proof membranes in older buildings. Today, their durability, coupled with their attractive colour and texture, means that they are still a welcome asset in the home.

Until rail transportation made its widespread use possible, slate flooring was once limited to installation in homes near working quarries. Today, however, we benefit from global improvements in both transportation and cutting machinery, bringing new colours of slate from India and China into the stock of materials available. These imported slates possess colours that were previously valued as extremely rare, such as soft greens and blues with coppery threads; these are now available at a price comparable to that of carpet when the materials are imported direct to retail outlets. This can prove to be a very sensible investment as slate flooring could outlive the house.

Slate's durability also means that it is possible to buy reclaimed flags from demolished buildings. Such material is worth considering for those renovating historical buildings, but bear in mind that reclaimed slate flags will be two or three times thicker than today's 10mm ($^{3}/_{8}$in) flags and should therefore be used only for downstairs rooms. Today's thin-cut slate flags serve more as tiling, and can be laid onto a level plywood sub-floor in upstairs rooms. With their hues of polished graphite, they look especially chic in bathrooms. Rarer colours from quarries in the Middle East offer such luscious colours as rich maroon, but these will, needless to say, be accompanied by a designer price tag. Still, used as a decorative accent, they can lend real power to a hard-wearing, water-resistant floor covering.

STONE FLAGS

In centuries past, stone floors were to be found not just in great architectural structures, but in modest dwellings also. Stone was a ubiquitous building material, its natural hues defining the character of regions from town to town and country to country.

The most common types of stone used for flooring are limestone and sandstone. As a metamorphic rock, limestone is difficult to split but extremely hardwearing. Created over thousands of years from the compression of calcified bones and other matter, it is often randomly decorated with small fossils, giving it a precious patina. When limestone is honed, its surface becomes very smooth, which, like that of marble, helps improve the stone's porosity.

Sandstone, on the other hand, is a sedimentary rock, formed in layers by the activity of water. It is easily split, therefore, but this separation leaves an attractive, riven, textured surface.

The great rustic limestone or sandstone flagstones that we see in old buildings today are often dark in colour, but this is because the only protection or sealant that was available in the past was animal fat or beeswax. These coatings certainly helped to prevent water, dirt and stains from penetrating the stone but they have also left a legacy of grime on the surface. The use of limestone and sandstone flags would have been confined to downstairs rooms, due to their thickness and weight, which needed solid foundations for support.

Limestone, with its soft hues and natural veining, possesses much of the beauty of marble, but can be bought today at around half the price of the latter. Laid in a classical grid, or offset with randomly sized setts, it is suitable for any room. Installation in a kitchen may not be ideal, since limestone is vulnerable to attack by acids such as wine and vinegar. However, today's silicon-based acrylic sealants will protect it from damage without damaging its colour or tone.

Although most sandstones are inert, and are not therefore damaged by acids, the molecular structure of the sand particles does make it more porous, so that grease and food debris can become ingrained. For this reason, sandstone is not a particularly suitable flooring material for hard-working kitchens, but it is perfect for creating a baronial hallway or grand dining or living room.

Stone flags are generally laid with a 3–5mm (⅛in) joint, which is filled with grout. It is important to keep these joints narrow, since large tracts of grout will wear and crack over the years, unlike the stone flags, which will last forever. Stone flags are difficult to lay, and it is advisable to call in a professional to do the job.

ABOVE: Although a traditional building material, sandstone flags here add a geometric pace to the floor of this modern kitchen. Their light gold colour provides an understated background to the bold blocks of colour of the kitchen units.

RIGHT: A sealed and polished stone flag floor, decorated only with a simple motif of diametric keystone insets, strikes an Art Deco note in a formal lobby that glows with restrained elegance.

OPPOSITE: The pale, natural tones of limestone flags possess a sensual as well as an architectural appeal and a look that can easily be translated into a modern building. The introduction of keystone insets adds a subtly decorative touch.

TERRACOTTA FLAGS AND TILES

Fired clay tiles are found in buildings dating back to Roman times, paving the floors of homes around the world, from humble English cottages to the elegant haciendas of Spain and lavish chateaux of France. With earthy hues ranging from honey-golds to fiery reds, they were the simplest building material available. Originally, they were made on site in wood-fired kilns that created a softly coloured, variegated tile, as the heat was low and uneven in its distribution. Tile colours also vary greatly, of course, depending on the source of the original clay. Later, in the 19th century, coal-fired kilns were used to produce a more uniform tile, and today the use of gas-fired kilns means that rich, evenly coloured tiles can be efficiently manufactured.

The word terracotta literally means 'fired earth', and clay tiles are made from unrefined clay that is fired in moulds. Quarry tiles are fired at very high temperatures, forcing out all the air in the clay to create a hard vitreous tile that is cold to the touch. Terracotta tiles are fired at lower temperatures so that some of the air in the clay mix remains. These small pockets of air help the tile to retain the ambient temperature of a room. There is nothing cosier than a terracotta-tiled floor in a rustic kitchen heated by an Aga – the guaranteed recipe for a room where everyone will want to congregate.

OPPOSITE: Variegated tones in the natural clay emerge during the firing process of terracotta tiles because of the uneven distribution of heat in the kiln at low temperatures. A bright, spiky border enlivens the somewhat muted effect.

LEFT: A dynamic geometric design has been created with tiles produced from contrasting pale and dark clays; the design is counterpointed with jewel-like, glazed blue ceramic tiles for a dramatic, contemporary tiled floor.

BELOW: The worn and pitted patina of antique terracotta tiles makes them an attractive choice for 'new' flooring in the homes of today. Laid in a simple square-set pattern, they still bring a cachet of character, warmth and charm.

Antique tiles can be bought from salvage companies and are well worth looking for: terracotta tiles are slightly softer than ceramic, so they usually have an attractive worn and pitted surface.

Terracotta tiles are usually laid square set, but patterns of running bonds or diagonal squares are also popular. The ideal base for laying terracotta tiles is a concrete screed, but they can also be laid on floorboards strengthened with marine ply screwed to the floor, with an expansion gap of about 12mm ($\frac{1}{2}$in) left around the edges.

The tiles can easily be laid with a cement-base adhesive or on mortar, with 5mm ($\frac{1}{8}$in) joints for grouting. Terracotta tiles are porous and need sealing to protect them from stains and spillages. They can be finished with boiled linseed oil worked over with a clean rag and then polished with wax when dry. There are also many proprietary sealants and finishes on the market to protect terracotta tiles.

MARBLE FLOORS

Often considered to be the most precious of flooring materials, marble is romantically associated with palaces as well as being used commercially for dramatic effect in civic and corporate buildings. Marble is a metamorphic rock that is inherently cool and, for this reason, it is widely used in Mediterranean countries to help keep interior temperatures low. The development of underfloor heating, however, means that marble can now be used in colder climates too.

Valued for the soft veins that run through its composition, marble creates a floor that is always unique: the pattern displayed in any individual piece of marble will never be repeated by nature. Traditionally, marble is polished to give it a glossy sheen, which is achieved with varying degrees of abrasive sanding. This polish does help to give marble a resistance to water, but the gleam can be overpowering in an ordinary domestic context.

A modern technique for creating marble tiles with a more muted, natural finish has been developed. Known as 'tumbled marble', it is produced by turning marble tiles in a machine with sand, water and granite. The machine tosses these about, much like clothes in a tumble dryer, removing sharp corners, creating a matt finish and leaving them with a pleasant, artificially aged effect.

Marbles are commonly available in a classic palette of colours. Pink and black marbles are quarried in Portugal, reds and greys in Italy and Spain, whites and creams in Italy and Greece, while greens are now imported from India and China. Scratches will, in fact, show

LEFT: From workspace to lounge living, the softly reflective sheen of a marble floor maximises light to create a feeling of luxurious spaciousness, as in this airy kitchen. The addition of a carpet in the living area instantly identifies the comfort zone.

OPPOSITE LEFT: Diagonally laid marble tiles with simple keystone insets, create a cool conservatory mood in a traditonal Victorian setting. Once sealed with a suitable product, a marble floor is durable and easy to maintain.

OPPOSITE RIGHT: Edwardian-style fixtures are complemented by a floor of black marble floor tiles, cut in small square sets and laid within a geometric black and onyx border that is echoed in the diagonally placed wall-border.

less on light-coloured marbles, since a scratch on black or green marble will show up as an unpolished white cut.

Marble tiles are now cut to a depth of 10mm ($^3/_8$in) and laid with a 2mm ($^1/_8$in) joint. It is easiest to lay the tiles on a plastic corrugated sheet, over a plywood sub-floor that is screwed to secure floorboards. The tiles are fixed in place with ceramic tile adhesive. Ensure that there are no pigments in the grout as these can leak into the marble. Grouts for shower floors should contain life-prolonging additives.

Marble is often thought of as a delicate floor covering, easily stained and difficult to clean. However, a new generation of excellent sealing products has now become available on the market and these make marble a much more viable option as a flooring material.

TERRAZZO FLOORING

Solid marble floors have a grand and opulent character, but their sheer smoothness can become monotonous. Texture and pattern can be introduced, however, by setting marble pieces in a compound to create an entirely new, more informal flooring material. Terrazzo is made from chips of marble set in either concrete or resin, the speckled flecks suggesting the texture of cut stone.

Commonly seen in Italy and other Mediterranean countries, terrazzo flooring has the attributes of other hard-flooring services, offering a sheer expanse of floor that is easy to maintain with only sweeping and wiping. It can be covered with rugs and carpets for warmth, while remaining practical and easy to clean.

Terrazzo is often bought in tiles and laid in much the same way as flags. However, the tiles can be obtained in larger sizes, often double the size of flags, and when the joints are filled with matching resin, the look is seamless. The finish is always smooth and polished, like the traditional surface of marble, which makes it more appropriate to modern interiors or for those interested in creative design: the polished finish does not lend itself to rustic, country-style interiors.

LEFT: Small pebbles set into concrete evoke the seashore, bringing a fresh outdoor mood to this room. This type of terrazzo treatment is ideal for a room that is linked to the exterior of a house, such as a conservatory or porch.

OPPOSITE ABOVE: A cut-out dolphin motif adds a witty touch to the terrazzo flag floor in this bathroom. Composite flooring, such as this, has a random pattern, creating the look of scattered mosaic. With its base of concrete or resin, it is particularly suitable for bathrooms.

OPPOSITE BELOW: The deep polish of a terrazzo floor is a common feature in Mediterraean homes, bringing a modern approach to the classic marble flooring of hot climates. Such flooring is extremely strong, though less cool than natural marble or stone.

Terrazzo can also be laid in situ with a trowel, in much the way that traditional scagliola was set: when it is worked in this way, fascinating designs and patterns are within the possibilities of the material. Other interesting materials, such as stone chips, can be introduced into the compound when terrazzo is being worked directly onto the floor, creating a variety of interesting textures.

Because the marble chips are set into a concrete, cement or resin base, terrazzo flooring is incredibly strong but is not necessarily as cool as natural marble or stone finishes. It is most usually seen in commercial or civic buildings, in foyers and lobbies, but it is increasingly being specified by architects working in converted commercial and industrial premises, transforming these huge, disused spaces into highly desirable, contemporary living quarters.

FAUX MARBLE FLAGS

A plain wooden, concrete or stone floor can be transformed into an opulent, palatial backdrop by painting it to look like marble. The paint is applied in rather ad hoc fashion, laying rough base layers and working into it until the required finish is achieved. It is a surprisingly simple technique, calling for no precision or careful application, yet the end result is absolutely stunning. Any colours can be used, but the most effective results come from sticking to colours that are found in nature, such as greens, browns and blues.

1 Prepare the floor surface by sanding it smooth and removing any dirt, dust or grease with white spirit. Apply two coats of beige floor paint with a masonry roller, allowing each coat to dry thoroughly. In three separate pots, mix the following shades of artist's oil colour with an equal quantity of white spirit: cobalt blue, raw sienna and terra verde. Working in small areas of approximately one square metre at a time, and using a large stipple brush, roughly paint on equal amounts of each colour in irregular patches.

2 Pull small pieces from the surface and edges of a synthetic household sponge. Soak the sponge in white spirit and squeeze out the excess. While the paint is still wet, pat the dampened sponge gently over the painted patches, softly merging the colours together. As you work across the surface, turn the sponge at different angles to prevent any regular patterns or hard edges marring the surface. The sponge will become slightly muddy, but this will simply add to the distribution of the colours.

3 Keep working the paint until there are no harsh borders between colours, but avoid over-blending: gentle pools of the original colours should remain. To create the mottling, dip an artist's brush in white spirit and spatter onto the paint by tapping the brush on a second brush handle. Wait for a minute while the paint disperses. Continue this process, allowing the white spirit to take effect before applying more. When the floor is suitably mottled, allow it to dry overnight then seal with a protective gloss varnish.

SCAGLIO FLOORING

Bend down to touch the most exquisitely laid 'marble' floors in some of the finest houses of the 18th century, and you may be surprised to feel a warmth that betrays the true character of the floor. This is not a painted effect: the polish and honing is authentic. The floor is most likely to be constructed of scagliola, one of the finest faux materials ever developed. Scagliola was first used to imitate marble, but because of its ability to create more decorative and ornate designs than was possible with the original material before the introduction of machine cutters, it became preferred to the authentic article. Scagliola was used extensively in the Palladian-style houses of the 18th century. Palladian architecture drew on classical architecture, embellishing the pure forms with classical ornamentation, and scagliola proved to have just the qualities to provide such decoration.

Old recipes for scagliola comprised boiled and sifted gypsum, mixed until it had the consistency of plaster, and then spread about 130mm (5in) thick on floors. Cavities were then made and filled with more scagliola mixed with dry pigments. This technique allowed for the creation of beautiful inlaid patterns that were then

LEFT: Detail of a floor from the Sheik of Abu-Dhabi's residence, Tittenhurst Park near Ascot. Scagliola was at first used to imitate marble, but its ability to create more decorative and ornate designs than the original material, meant it became preferable to the authentic article.

OPPOSITE ABOVE: Scagliola floor detail from a private house in London. Scagliola is worked today, using plaster of Paris mixed with water and dry pigments. Coloured plaster is kneaded together with plain plaster to create the fine thread-vein streaks that characterise marble.

OPPOSITE BELOW: Syon House. Scagliola was used extensively in the Palladian-style houses of the 18th century. Palladian architecture drew on classical architecture, embellishing the pure forms with classical ornamentation, and scagliola proved to have just the qualities for such decoration.

sanded and polished smooth. In this way, beautiful faux black and white marble floors were produced, as well as highly decorative floors that were coloured in imitation of other, more precious stones.

Original scagliola flooring has survived amazingly well and, where damage has occurred, the crumbling plaster can be successfully repaired with a new mixture of scagliola carefully prepared to match the original colouring – a task that is somewhat easier than attempting to match new marble to old.

Scagliola is still worked today using plaster of Paris mixed with water and dry pigments. Coloured plaster is kneaded together with plain plaster to create the fine thread-vein streaks that characterize marble. After the scagliola has been sanded back to an even surface, it is then oiled and waxed to produce a fine sheen.

CONTEMPORARY CONCRETE

Being considered an unsightly workhorse – the load-bearing sub-floor with sub-standard aesthetic appeal – concrete is generally relegated to its functional place, below more decorative floor surfaces. This 20th-century mix of cement, sand, stone and water is too often associated with the soulless, grey, prefabricated buildings of the 1950s and 60s. Concrete floors are the stuff of the strip-lit factory, homes of heavy industry. Yet it is precisely this application that gives concrete its cue to enter the vocabulary of contemporary, domestic interior design.

In urban areas, there is a move now to reclaim disused industrial warehouses, those ghostly monuments to outmoded commercial enterprises. Individuals are effecting their own 'conversions', embracing the stark, utilitarian architecture along with their expanses of concrete flooring. As a result, concrete is enjoying a renaissance and it is now considered a suitably fashionable material for interiors wishing to capture the essence of the post-modern habitat.

Existing concrete floors can take on new, more colourful personalities with paint. Special floor paints are available that give concrete a wipeable coating, although these will chip and flake over time. It is easy, however, to simply paint concrete with a diluted water-based matt emulsion: the colour seeps into the concrete surface and will not chip or flake at all. This opens up the possibility of painting designs on concrete, from traditional patterns to urban graffiti or classically inspired 'fresco'. When dry, the floor can be finished with a modern silicon-based sealant as used for stone flooring.

Laying a new concrete screed is a cheap and easy job for any builder, and it is possible to experiment with the aggregate to form more pleasing hues than the bleak grey so often associated with concrete. White cement, containing lime, gives a softer look, while pigments can be added to introduce other colours to the mix.

Concrete paving tiles, once used exclusively outdoors, are now being introduced into interiors too, conveying a starkness and minimalism that echoes the Zen calm of Japanese interiors.

FLAGSTONES AND TILES

OPPOSITE: Concrete can work just as well in a rustic-style kitchen as in a stark modern interior. Here, a coat of blue-grey matt emulsion paint has been applied to concrete slabs to emulate the appearance of traditional slate flags.

LEFT: A contemporary slant on the classic chequerboard floor has been achieved here. Laid diagonally across the floor, the coloured concrete paviours are perfectly proportionate to the floor area in this converted industrial space.

BELOW: Concrete paviours line this coolly tranquil, Japanese-inspired bathroom. Concrete can be polished to give a lustrous finish that is perfectly suited to a clean, sleek, contemporary environment such as this.

CERAMIC TILES

Ceramic floor tiles can provide one of the most economical ways of creating a long-lasting, decorative and waterproof floor surface. They compare well in price per metre with vinyl floor coverings and budget carpets yet, if laid with care, they offer a more resilient and long-lasting floor surface than either of those options.

Ceramic tiles are made from clay dust, which is pressed into moulds then fired at high temperatures, resulting in a vitrified non-porous tile. This means they cannot retain heat and so are always cold to the touch. For this reason, ceramic tiles belong to the interior vocabulary of hotter climates. They are typically associated with Mediterannean countries, such as Italy and Spain, which have the largest markets for ceramic tiles.

Ceramic tiles are hard and brittle, so care should be taken in busy areas, such as kitchens, where a dropped cast-iron pan could easily smash a tile. Accidents can be repaired by carefully levering away the damaged tile and replacing it. Check also that tiles chosen for a kitchen have a suitable glaze that will not absorb oil or grease. Ceramic floor tiles are also made with an anti-slip specification.

LEFT: This highly decorative, glazed, ceramic tile floor is copied from the original 14th-century floor discovered intact at the Palace of the Popes in Avignon, France. Tiles with different motifs are interspersed with richly coloured plain tiles.

OPPOSITE LEFT: With cool, plain ceramic tiles, a white floor instantly becomes a viable option for this elegant dining room, where soft, white furnishings and paintwork contribute to the overall feeling of light-infused space.

OPPOSITE RIGHT: In this classic bathroom, pure white tiles with a black triangle at each corner are set square to form a black and white floor with what appears to be tiny black key insets. The tiling is continued in the raised shower area.

The most common application for ceramic tiles is, of course, in the bathroom where they offer a continuity with wall tiles to create a room protected by a wipeable, hygienic surface that is elegantly adapted to the ravages of daily ablutions. In the main, glazed ceramic tiles require little upkeep, as their glaze is sealant enough. For kitchens and bathrooms, an epoxy-based grout is often recommended for its waterproof properties and resistance to bacteria.

Most machine-made ceramic tiles can be cut and shaped with a hand-cutting tool, which means that their installation can be undertaken by a careful amateur. To achieve a professional finish, the tiles must be laid on a perfectly flat surface; careful setting out to find the centre point of the room must also be undertaken before starting work. The gaps between ceramic floor tiles are filled with grout, with any excess wiped off before it dries hard on the tile.

Many different shapes and patterns of ceramic tiles are avail-able. Richly decorative tiles can create a jewel-like floor, while plain tiles, punctuated occasionally by decorative feature tiles provide an understated charm. Perhaps some of the oldest patterned tile designs are the naive motifs of 17th-century Delft tiles. These are best known as a white ground with a blue character painted on each, although other colours were used too. Their tin glaze has given these tiles an attractive 'crackled' finish that new, commercial tiles now also imitate. Tiles such as these are ideal for use in a traditional context, such as a fireplace hearth, or as feature tiles in a country-style kitchen.

With functionality now becoming a key design priority, the easy-to-maintain surface of a ceramic floor means that tiles are now making their debut in living and dining rooms. An expanse of cream ceramic flooring is a classic look that will create the perfect canvas for a focus carpet or specially designed rug, while the reflective nature of the glaze adds light to interior spaces.

TRADITIONAL ENCAUSTIC TILES

Decoratively patterned unglazed tiles are generally associated with the entrance halls and conservatories of 19th-century Victorian interiors. Found in terraced houses, American brownstones and in the colonial homes of Empire, they became popular as part of a fascination with all things Gothic in architecture and the decorative arts. Geometric flooring patterns, made from ingenious combinations of coloured triangular, hexagonal and square feature tiles, are still commonly found in hallways today, as are more simple black and white diamond patterns. Encaustic tiles actually date back to a much earlier time, and are found as floor ornamentation in medieval churches and abbeys. They were hand-made by Cistercian monks in the 12th century, but the dissolution of the monastaries ended their efforts, and their manufacture was abandoned until the 19th century when the Victorians rediscovered the secrets of making these durable, decorative tiles.

Encaustic tiles are made by pressing soft red clay into a mould imprinted with pattern indentations. After the tile undergoes an initial firing, a coloured slip is poured into the indentation, and is fired again. Unlike painted tiles, the process ensures that the colour and pattern are fired throughout the tile and cannot be worn away.

Encaustic tiles require careful maintenance: wire wool or metal brushes must never be used on them, and beware of cleaning agents containing salts that may cause damage. Instead clean them with a 50:50 solution of white spirit and water mixed with two drops of washing up liquid. Apply liquid beeswax to the floor and leave to dry for 24 hours before buffing to a soft sheen.

OPPOSITE: The patterns adorning traditional encaustic tiles have their roots in the 12th century, when they were first made by Cistercian monks. The process was rediscovered and popularized by the Victorians in the 19th century.

ABOVE: The rich, geometric patterning of decorative encaustic tiles is commonly found in the entrance halls of Victorian and Edwardian homes, providing a characteristic welcome and a surface that is easy to clean and maintain.

RIGHT: A modern encaustic tile inset cleverly spices up a classic terracotta floor design. The simple folk motif complements perfectly the rustic flooring, while the matching grouting leads the eye from one motif to the next.

MODERN ENCAUSTIC TILES

Traditional, geometric encaustic tiles are still manufactured today by specialist companies, as are unglazed ceramic tiles that reproduce the original Victorian and Edwardian patterns of encaustic tiles. These tiles are, of course, ideal for those wishing to reinstate original features to a house in need of restoration. If laid new in kitchen areas, the tiles can be well protected with an impregnating sealer.

Beyond the traditional patterns painstakingly devised by 19th-century craftsmen, new designs of encaustic tiles are now being manufactured, though these are still produced in the traditional way. The slightly rough texture of the unglazed tiles gives them a quality and appearance that is similar to stone. Designers have exploited this similarity by creating primitive designs of stylized fossils that echo the natural imprints so valued in limestones and other rocks. Shapes devised from early religious symbols and early heraldic motifs can also be found, all fired in the more natural slips of buff-creams, earth-reds and blacks. These designs are ideal for creating a more imaginitive and personalized floor design. Mingled among quarry tiles or terracotta tiles, they add pace and quirky interest to plain squares, and their folk-art style fits in well with the rustic texture of fired clay tiles. Though they are expensive, when used in this way only a few patterned tiles are needed to add a distinctive touch to an otherwise plain floor.

Because encaustic tiles are unglazed, they are especially compatible with terracotta floor tiles and quarry tiles and can work wonderfully well when incorporated into an overall flooring scheme, either randomly or in a repeat pattern; the designs will be as long-lasting and hardwearing as their larger partners as their production ensures that the pattern is fired throughout the tile.

There is no reason – apart from perhaps the cost – why such decorative tiles cannot be used to create a complete floor, rather than being used only as insets: the effect would be one of decorative fantasy, similar to the designs of trompe l'oeil mosaics. Unless used in an otherwise minimal interior, the effect could be rather overwhelming.

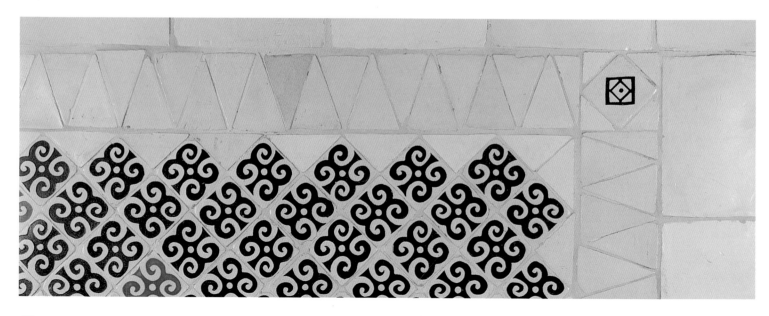

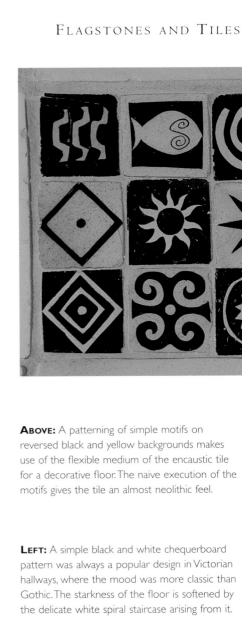

ABOVE: A patterning of simple motifs on reversed black and yellow backgrounds makes use of the flexible medium of the encaustic tile for a decorative floor. The naive execution of the motifs gives the tile an almost neolithic feel.

LEFT: A simple black and white chequerboard pattern was always a popular design in Victorian hallways, where the mood was more classic than Gothic. The starkness of the floor is softened by the delicate white spiral staircase arising from it.

OPPOSITE: An early Etruscan feel is captured in a milky coloured decorative floor of encaustic tiles, given graphic gravitas with its repeated black motif patterning, contained within a self-coloured border of simple triangular shapes.

MOSAIC FLOORS

Mosaics stand alone as the most intricate and visually arresting of floor treatments. In close proximity, the tiny tesserae – small cut tiles that constitute the pattern – fascinate the eye with their detail, while from a distance they meld to create designs that appear almost three-dimensional. Many ancient mosaic pavements exploited this potential with imaginative trompe l'oeil designs.

Mosaic floors give an impression of opulence and perhaps it is for this reason that their main application is as a choice of flooring for bathrooms, where indulgence and luxury take equal place with the practicality afforded by their resistance to water damage.

Hallways are another key location for mosaic flooring, where ostentatious touches are permissable. Enthusiasm should be countered, however, by the size of the home: it is often more effective to choose just a mosaic inset for a porch or doorway, or to add a border of mosaic to a flagstone floor, than to construct a complete mosaic floor. Limestone tesserae, for example, create a stunning architectural feature in a simple limstone-paved floor. Mosaic floors are there to be seen, which makes them inappropriate for rooms that need the additional warmth of rugs that conceal their beauty.

Ancient mosaics were made from hand-cut marble or stone, embedded on a lime mortar. In the 19th century, a technique was developed whereby large pictorial tiles were manufactured with deep grooves; once the tiles were laid, the grooves were grouted to imitate a complete mosaic floor.

Today, tesserae can be hand- or machine-cut, although a finished mosaic with smooth machine-cut tesserae will lack the definition of a hand-cut mosaic. The smallest, and therefore more expensive, unit of tessarae is 1 square cm ($\frac{3}{8}$in), with the average size being 1.5 square cm ($\frac{5}{8}$in) and the largest never usually being larger than 2 square cm ($\frac{3}{4}$in). It is now a less laborious task to have a mosaic floor installed, as the mosaicist does not have to work in situ but assembles the pattern onto a fibre backing with adhesive, usually in 28-square-cm (11in) sections. Each section is then belaid with latex adhesive either onto a concrete sub-floor or, in the case of upstairs bathrooms, onto a floor made level with 2cm (1in) marine plywood screwed to wooden floorboards at 10cm (5in) intervals. Grooves are then infilled with a sand and cement grout, and the floor can be finished with an appropriate stone or marble sealant.

Mosaics can be created from other materials: pebbles, coloured ceramic or pre-cut glass 'smalti' tiles; or, when laid in small areas such as a hearth or doorstep, they can be fashioned from recycled stone or china for a more folk-art look.

ABOVE: Glazed ceramic tesserae in a rich lapis-blue colour recreate the visual rhythm of water in this elegant bathroom. A curvilinear thread of cream in the mosaic floor echoes the curving lines of the cabinet in which the basin is inset.

LEFT: Natural stone mosaics offer a subtle palette of colour for delicate, naturalistic patterns such as these. The soft sheen of limestone tesserae are often preferable to a gleaming display of marble for domestic interiors.

OPPOSITE: There has long been a connection between water and the art of the mosaicist whose skills were regularly employed to adorn Roman baths – themselves the inspiration for many of today's bathrooms.

FAUX MOSAIC DESIGNS

The timeless art of mosaic provides the ultimate interest on a floor yet, in practice, it is a skilled and time-consuming job that few non-professionals would relish tackling. Fortunately, the same tessellated effect can be achieved in a fraction of the time and at minimum cost, using paint and home-made print blocks to create faux mosaic designs on a wooden, stone or concrete floor. Different blocks can be combined to add interest, using a basic grid for the main floor and a border design in a contrasting colour as shown here.

1 Sand the floor and clean it with white spirit to remove traces of dirt. Apply two coats of beige floor paint with a masonry roller; allow the paint to dry thoroughly between coats. Measure the dimensions of the floor area and divide it into equal sections approximately 12 x 20cm (5 x 8in) to give an exact size for your printing block. Draw a repeat border motif onto tracing paper, working to the same width as your main block but twice the length; simple, neatly linking patterns with a plain border on either side of the repeat motif work best. Cut the blocks from 2cm- (¾in) thick solid foam rubber.

2 Draw a grid onto the main block with squares measuring approximately 2.5 x 2.5cm (1 x 1in). Using a sharp craft knife, cut out the lines to roughly 2mm (⅛in) in width, keeping them as even as possible and gouging no deeper than half the thickness of the block. Transfer the traced border motif onto the border block and cut out the pattern, removing any loose pieces of rubber. Paint the border colours in gloss paint onto the relief border block, taking care not to mix the colours. Lay the main block in one corner of the room and begin applying the border from this point, adding more paint as necessary.

3 Move the block along, positioning it accurately so that the pattern matches. Allow the border to dry. To apply the main grid, paint the main block with orange gloss paint then daub the relief pattern with red to add more texture. Match the grid block to the corner of the border and begin printing. As you move the block along, twist it 90° to give a random distribution of any irregularities in the pattern. When the main floor is complete, clean the grid block and paint with the colours of the corner tiles. Print the corner tiles and leave the floor to dry overnight. Seal the pattern with two coats of acrylic varnish.

CARPETS, RUGS AND COVERINGS

For comfort and warmth in a cold climate, carpets and rugs offer stylish ways to develop the decorative dimension of a room. Textile coverings literally warm a floor, sealing draughts and insulating against heat loss, as well as providing softness under foot and absorbing noise.

For sheer sensual luxury, a wool carpet reigns supreme. Plain carpets give a neutral background that can create unity and a sense of space when fitted throughout a house. Patterned carpets, on the other hand, offer scope to the decorator, who can choose from sprigs, pin-dots, heraldic motifs, linear, geometrics and a wealth of border pattterns.  Versatile and adaptable, rugs can be used on all floors. Kelims and oriental carpets complement both modern and traditional interiors, whereas painted floor canvases protect and adorn floors in a simple, fresh way.

While adventurous designers are exploring new mediums for floor coverings, from paper to leather, the vast choice of rugs, runners and floor coverings now available in natural fibres, such as coir, echo the dawn of the covered floor, when simple rushes and matting were used.

CARPETS

Warm and gentle, soft and sensual, carpet is perhaps the most indulgent of all floor coverings. For those with a young family, it is probably the only choice for living rooms and bedrooms, where it provides unrivalled comfort for sensitive young toes.

Today there have been so many advances in carpet technology that it is almost impossible to buy a 'bad' carpet. Even on a low budgets, it is possible to buy a perfectly serviceable carpet. Cheaper carpets offer good wear, though they will not continue to look as good over the years as more expensive alternatives. Experts agree that the worst thing a customer can do is to buy the wrong carpet for the job, such as laying a light domestic carpet in a heavy traffic area.

Carpets are made either of wool or of man-made fibres – or a mixture of both. Wool carpets are less prone to static, with low flammability and good resistance to soiling. Wool is inherently strong and is considered the most hard-wearing fibre for carpets. Mixed fibre carpets are popular as their content of coal- or oil-derived synthetic fibres substantially increases their durability.

There are two classic methods of wool-carpet construction. Wilton is a woven carpet with a velvet pile or a looped pile, known as Brussels weave. Axminster carpet, another traditional woven carpet, has tufts inserted between every two rows of weft threads.

Fitted carpets became readily available only after the Second World War when the increasingly widespread use of the broad loom produced carpets in 2.7m (8.8ft) widths. Coupled with the development of synthetic fibre technology, a soft, insulating, sound-proofing, draught-excluding floor covering became affordable for all.

The ultimate expression of this advancement is a sheer expanse of plain-coloured fitted carpet. Continuing from one room to the next, it suggests both unity and luxury, as pattern is not required to disguise wear. Plain carpets are usually tufted carpets, and today's stain-inhibiting systems can prolong their wear considerably. When used in a room on their own, without the addition of rugs, plain carpets can help to create an impression of space: the borders left around rugs can visually shrink a room to the limits of those borders.

When choosing a plain carpet, basic colour principles should be considered, along with existing colour schemes and personal preferences. Light colours brighten and enlarge small dark rooms, while dark shades can make a large room feel more cosy. Reddish tones or sunny yellows will warm a cold, north-facing room, while sunny rooms can be cooled with greens and blues.

OPPOSITE: A bedroom with few windows and little daylight can create its own ambience of warmth and welcome with a spicy red tufted carpet to complement the soft yellow walls and richly coloured bed coverings.

LEFT: A mellow peach tone sets the right mood of brightness and warmth in this welcoming family living room. Carpet is ideal for crawling infants and unsteady toddlers, protecting them from bumps and providing a comfortable place to play.

BELOW: A modern living room is given an architectural theme with the colour of the walls matched by the expanse of soft mushroom-white carpet. The plain, neutral carpeting increases the room's feeling of airy spaciousness.

TEXTURES AND SMALL-SCALE PATTERNS

With the invention of the tufting manufacturing process, carpets became more widely accessible to all homes. The looms used in the process were originally developed to produce candlewick bedspreads, but this was then extended to carpet-making. The tufts are simply hooked through a backing material then secured with an adhesive. Attempts at replicating the large patterns of traditional Axminsters were not so successful with tufting, however, and it was found that smaller-scale patterns could be achieved more easily.

In recent years, decorators and designers have sought more understated patterns in carpets, in contrast to the large, overblown excesses of the carpet boom of the 1970s. Small pin-dots have become more widely used and offer a mid-point compromise between minimalist plains and traditional, large-patterned carpets. Small patterns still serve the purpose of helping to disguise the inevitable staining or wear that can occur, while allowing the dominant ground colour to take centre stage. Simple flower sprigs are ideal for bedrooms and take their inspiration from the delicate tapestries of the 18th and 19th centuries. Geometric lozenges are also popular, as are small heraldic motifs, such as fleur-de-lis and laurel wreaths, associated with the 18th-century French Empire style. These are suited to everday rooms such as living rooms, dining rooms and studies.

Pattern can also be introduced to plain carpets in the form of texture. Some attractive and creative designs have been produced in this area of carpet manufacture, largely as a response to the popularity of natural fibre carpets. Natural fibre carpets are favoured more for the interest of their weave than the beauty of the material. Wool carpets have attempted to imitate this effect with varying degrees of success. Initially the result was rather flat and lifeless, whereas wool or wool blends are admired for their springiness and life. It is now possible, however, to buy wool carpets with attractive bouclé weaves that possess the aesthetic appeal of natural fibre carpets yet still have the softness underfoot that makes wool carpet so covetable.

An increasing market has developed for carpets that mix natural fibres with wool mixes, and these can serve as a good compromise in living rooms where a degree of toughness and comfort is sought.

For extra texture, deep-tufted, shag-pile carpets are also making a comeback as elements of 20th century design are re-introduced and celebrated. The deep sensual folds of shag-pile carpet beneath the toes is, of course, something of a luxury status product – keeping white shag-pile clean is only possible for those who are well housetrained. Such attributes, along with a pinch of post-modern irony, have encouraged its resurrection in bedrooms and living rooms alike.

ABOVE: Wool carpets, such as this, are now designed as a flat weave rather than a twisted or tufted covering, offering softness underfoot in bedrooms while, at the same time, suggesting the rustic mood of more rough-hewn materials.

LEFT: The large flat weave of this wool carpet is evocative of a honeycomb, and brings its own subtle patterning to a plain floor covering. The colour is warm and glowing and fits easily into the sun-dappled mood of the room.

OPPOSITE: A waffle-wave weave introduces texture to a plain, biscuit-coloured carpet, giving an earthy look that blends well with the combination of ethnic and modern furnishings in this homely living room.

79

BOLD-PATTERNED CARPETS

Boldly patterned carpets bring a rich decorative ambience to a room. They give an impression of grandeur and, for this reason, they are best suited to living rooms, hallways and dining rooms. A patterned carpet is a wise choice for areas of heavy traffic, as the inevitable spills, accidents and general wear and tear will show much less on darker patterns, thus increasing the life of the carpet. This in-built advantage of patterned carpet over plain may well be a deciding factor in the final choice of what is inevitably a major expense.

Traditional Axminster carpets are generally associated with patterned designs. In the 19th century, these woven, tufted carpets imitated the exotic formations of Persian carpets in rich reds, greens and blues. These designs have since become classics and are still available and very popular today. However, while the Victorians lavished patterns on every surface, from floors to walls to ceilings, a more balanced mood can be created for our more sensitive tastes by combining patterned carpets with plain walls, so that the carpet itself becomes the decorative focus of the room.

Tartans and plaids are also designs associated with the 19th

LEFT: A large, boldly coloured plaid carpet gives a traditional, masculine feel to this workroom. Plain walls, which pick up on a minor colour in the plaid, counterbalance the carpet's richness, allowing it to take centre stage.

OPPOSITE ABOVE: Vivid, indigo-blue fitted carpet, matching the paintwork on the dado in both the adjacent living room and the stairwell, contributes magnificently to the vibrant feel of this simple yet bold interior.

OPPOSITE BELOW: The simplest, most subtle point of departure for carpet pattern – regular, small insets of complementary colour – leads the eye round the room and through the house, with a restful feeling of unity and continuity.

century, yet such carpets have found a place in contemporary interiors, providing a more restrained, less ornate pattern, which are ideal for both country-style interiors and smart town-house decoration.

Flat-weave carpets have undergone something of a renaissance, with mills in the highlands of Scotland once again producing carpets in tweeds and colourful plaids that can be used as elegant floor coverings – though a skilled fitter would be needed to ensure that these were laid successfully, with correctly matching patterns. These carpets would not be suitable for heavy traffic areas, unless loose laid as rugs, but they do make successful 'runners' in hallways.

Associated, perhaps, with naturalistic patterns from Victorian pattern books, modern and abstract designs are now becoming accepted in everyday domestic settings, contributing a fresh, contemporary look. Wilton carpets are not generally associated with patterns, but some of the finest bespoke carpets are Wiltons, often woven with a Brussels loop weave to give the design a clearer definition.

DECORATIVE BORDERS

As a design tool, borders help to contain the pattern on a carpet or rug by ascribing a clean edge. At the same time, they evoke the look of traditionally woven rugs and tapestries, which were finished with taped edges. Expanses of plain, unpatterned carpet can be given definition by borders, especially in room schemes where the floor and wall colours match. The border sets the boundaries, giving a more tailored look to a room. By adding a frame to a room, however, borders can diminish the proportions of a smaller room, so consideration should be given to the room's size before deciding.

Borders with patterns cut into the pile are widely available and are an ideal way of introducing finishing touches without interrupt-

ing the flow of a colour or pattern. Borders can be used to emphasize architectural features, such as a hearth or bay window, or to create a visual division between different areas – for example, between a dining area and the living room.

It is possible, with a bespoke carpet, to have the border woven in as part of the complete design, but the most affordable method is to have a border stitched to the carpet. If the latter method is followed, it is important to use felt underlay when the carpet is fitted, as a rubber underlay on its own will not help the seams to bed down.

Larger carpet companies are now producing borders that can be easily stuck to the main body of carpet with strong adhesive tape

OPPOSITE LEFT: A wide, plain, richly coloured border is inset into a pale carpet, helping to make the floor seem larger rather than visually reducing it. The room has an effortless unity, with the border colour matching that of the walls.

OPPOSITE RIGHT: A traditional border finishes a classic carpet, much as a gilded frame sets off a painted canvas on a wall, and creates a look of timless elegance that is the perfect backdrop to fine furniture and gracious living.

RIGHT: A border can be treated as a carpet accessory, offering the opportunity to impose individual ideas and style on a plain, functional carpet. Changing the look with fashion-led designs can add distinctive charm to a room.

— a job that is done in situ by the carpet fitter. This has meant that interior designers can now play around with fashion and novelty, creating border accessories that include novelties such as animal print designs with an Art Deco feel. Young funky interiors will benefit from zebra prints and the like, as long as it isn't overdone: matching rugs would confuse the issue, but sensitively done the eye will be drawn to a playfulness on the boundaries of the floor line.

Equally arresting are plaid borders and floral motifs that can look like a pretty embroidered ribbon edging. Approached with a spirit of inventiveness, a border edging can shift the focus of flooring in fresh and interesting ways. The wide choice of borders available opens up exciting possibilities for adding your own stamp to a carpet, ensuring that it becomes an integral part of your interior design plan rather than a necessary but undistinguished afterthought.

LINOLEUM AND VINYL

One of the greatest flooring innovations of the 20th century was the introduction of man-made floor coverings such as linoleum. Possessing the virtues of soft carpet, durable tiles and stone and warm, yielding wood, these materials have the additional advantage of resistance to water, making them the most practical choice for kitchens and bathrooms for the past 100 years.

Linoleum was invented in 1863 by Frederic Walton to a recipe of natural materials, including flax and linseed oil, that has changed little today. Indeed, the name comes from the two Latin words *lino* (flax) and *oleum* (oil). The resulting tough floor sheeting or tiles with a tough hessian backing has pigments added to produce a wide range of colour options. Some 60 colours are now available from the companies who manufacture linoleum.

Known for its marbled pattern or, in earlier documents, with spatter paint effects, linoleum enjoyed a boom of application during the post-war years; it is now enjoying a renaissance as a flooring classic, helped by its inherent bactericidal and hypo-allergenic properties. Unlike carpet, linoleum will not harbour dust mites or germs in the home, thus ensuring its popularity in the kitchen as well as in the bedrooms and nurseries of allergy-conscious households.

Vinyl coverings have also played a key role in furnishing the floors of utility areas in the 20th century. Cushioned vinyls contain a layer of foam, ensuring a comfortable 'give' underfoot, while still providing an easily wipeable surface. Also available are luxury floor vinyls made from polyvinyl chloride (PVC), which is manufactured to produce highly sophisticated simulations of slate, stone and wooden floors, with appropriately textured surfaces. Fantasy floor coverings are now being produced, with the latest designs showing camera-real images of meadow grass, sandy beaches or shallow water pools.

LEFT: Soft, warm underfoot and available in a refreshing choice of designs and colours, vinyl is an affordable and practical choice with the needs of a young family in mind. Its easy wipeability makes it an ideal for kitchens and dining areas.

OPPOSITE: Demonstrating that man-made floor coverings have a place in the most elegant and sophisticated of interiors, this smooth expanse of flooring with its cool, clean tiles is crossed by a 'walkway' between two distinct living areas.

INSETS, TILES AND BORDERS

Linoleum and vinyl floor coverings are normally laid over a latex screed to ensure that the sub-floor is absolutely level. This prevents the rucking or bubbling that used to happen in the early days of sheet linoleum and resulted in tears. The latex screed can either cover a concrete floor or be laid over plywood screwed down to existing floor boards. The floor covering is then best secured with a synthetic rubber-emulsion adhesive. Bear in mind, however, that luxury vinyls with a depth of 2.5mm ($\frac{1}{8}$in) or more are best fitted by a professional.

Linoleum and vinyl are sold in both sheet and tile form. Sheet flooring comes in large widths, which means it can often be laid without the need for a seam. However, if a join is required, thought should be given to where it is positioned, avoiding areas of high traffic, where tears can catch, or at a focal point in the room.

Vinyl and linoleum floor tiles are well suited for creating floor designs that imitate the marbled floors of 18th century homes – for example to produce classic chequerboard patterns in rooms such as

LEFT: A central inset and matching border design create the mood of a large carpet with a distinctly contemporary look in this easy-to-maintain flooring. Soft colours, with fresh, clean associations, blend easily into the living space.

OPPOSITE LEFT: Rich colours create added drama with a marbled form of linoleum that adds a warm patina to the background colour. Following the lines of the room, the border picks up on one of the colours in the central inset.

OPPOSITE RIGHT: A classic floor pattern finds new expression in a different medium: linoleum tiles may not as be durable as real flags, but they do have the comfort factor and are ideally suited to areas where water spillage is a possibility.

kitchens or bathrooms, which are not normally considered worthy of the expense of the real thing. For a charming country feel, you might like to create a gingham effect with a design that uses clear background tiles, contrasting coloured tiles and mid-tone marble tiles.

Tiles come in standard sizes but they can also be cut to make smaller tiles; however, the longevity of the floor may be slightly reduced with the use of smaller tiles as they inevitabley have more seams that can be penetrated by water spillages. Despite the good resistance to water of these floorings, seams are a vulnerable spot where water penetration may damage the adhesive bond.

Linoleum is receiving much more creative attention these days, which means that there is no reason why it can't be used in living spaces where it can be viewed and celebrated as an impressive design

medium. Its durability makes it an ideal choice for a young family that needs to take practical considerations on board, as well as wishing to maintain the design-conscious environment of more carefree days. But on a day-to-day basis, it is flooring that is easy to maintain, wipeable, and washable, with a flexibility that makes it a forgiving choice for the demands of a busy family home.

Linoleum and vinyl floors can be cleaned with warm water and a little detergent; this should be well rinsed to avoid a filmy build up. Since gritty abrasion damages the surface of vinyl, the floor should be brushed regularly. Once or twice a year, an acrylic floor-dressing product can be applied to improve wear; dressing applications that have built up over the years can be removed with a solution of one eggcupful of ammonia added to a bucket of cold to tepid water.

CUT PATTERNS

Today's linoleum and vinyl floor coverings have been commandeered by architects and designers to create floor designs that challenge and match the imagination and artistic beauty of some of the greatest stone, mosaic and wooden floors of history.

The expanse of colour offered by sheet flooring allows the introduction of pattern on a large scale. With materials such as stone and wood, designs have to be built up with smaller units; with carpet, while patterns can be woven and accentuated by cutting the pile, the design definition is not as clear as with vinyl or linoleum. There are

many companies who specialize in creating floor designs with the aid of computer technology, and these can generally be located by contacting the manufacturer.

The basic method of cutting vinyl or linoleum flooring is with a craft knife and, with some vinyl floor coverings, it is possible for the competent amateur to cope successfully with this. For complex designs, however, vinyl and linoleum are best cut by professionals.

For square tiles, a cutting die is used, which works on the principle of a guillotine. More complex patterns are either hand-cut or cut with an aquajet, a fine jet of very high-pressured water, guided by computer, that pushes out a fine line of vinyl or linoleum to separate shapes and templates from the main sheet. Specialist manufacturers, such as Amtico, have developed other computer-aided cutting devices

that do not even remove this fine line, thus giving a closer fit.

The use of these sophisticated cutting devices means that any shape or block of colour can be produced, giving more or less a free rein to the designer, much as if a pen or brush were being used. Even script or block writing can be inlaid, creating work that looks as if months were spent finely chiselling the design from stone or marble, while in fact it would have taken only minutes to devise. Photo-imaging technology has extended the possibilities even further.

Boundaries are constantly being pushed forward in the composition of the floorcovering too. Glitter designs, metal treadplate imitations … the innovations continue to add a vast spectrum of possibilities to design, making flooring options as excitingly diverse as those previously restricted to furnishing fabrics.

OPPOSITE LEFT: Advances in computer-aided design means that complicated cutting patterns can be produced in synthetic flooring materials. The delicate fan shapes in this radiating floor would be difficult to replicate in natural materials

OPPOSITE RIGHT: A design of voluptuously oversized fossil and leaf formations breaks up a large grid of marmoleum floor tiles, bringing exciting architectural detail to what would otherwise be a plain, functional kitchen.

RIGHT: A central mosaic-effect circular panel and a ribboned border employing similar geometric motifs continue the faux-classical impression of this stone-effect vinyl floor covering, which gives the feel of an elegant Mediterranean terrace.

CREATING CUT PATTERNS

Cut patterns can add a distinctive and individual look to a linoleum or vinyl floor. While simple geometric motifs are perhaps the easiest to cut, almost any design is possible. Cut patterns work particularly well when starting with a chequerboard tile base; the tiles are easy to work with, the checks add an extra design element and the two colours can be paired up to allow the cut shape from one to be slotted into the other. This allows for a direct exchange of pieces, which creates two cut patterns for the work of one.

1 Before you start, make sure that the floor is perfectly level and clean, removing any grease with white spirit. Lay out a chequerboard design of alternating black and white self-adhesive vinyl tiles to give you an idea of the overall effect. Mark the tiles that you want to cut and remove these from the floor, placing them in black and white pairs. Using a compass or a round object as a guide, draw a circle onto one tile of one pair.

2 Lay the tile to be cut on a cutting mat, or on a spare piece of board to protect the surface underneath. Using a sharp, heavy-duty craft knife, cut out the circle, in one piece, leaving the surrounding tile intact. Lay the cut-out circle onto the opposite-coloured tile of the pair and draw around it. Cut out this second circle. Slot each circle into the opposite-coloured surround to ensure that it fits snugly, trimming off any excess if necessary.

3 Mark out and cut the remaining pairs of tiles in the same way, varying the sizes and positions of the circles within the tiles. Beginning in the centre of the room, remove the backing paper from a tile and position it carefully, using a cloth to smooth it onto the floor and pressing firmly to ensure that it is completely stuck down. Lay the remaining tiles in the same way, laying the surrounds of the cut tiles first, before fitting the circles.

NATURAL FIBRE MATTING

Natural fibre matting harks back to the earliest domestic interiors. In its crudest form, grasses were strewn for warmth on cold castle floors while, in medieval homes, rushes were woven to make the first mats – an ancient craft that still thrives in the English county of Suffolk.

It is only in recent years, however, that floor coverings woven from natural fibres have entered the lexicon of interior design. These flat-weave floorings bring an earthy, raw aesthetic to interiors while still providing the familiar benefits of more sophisticated carpets. The popularity of natural fibre floor coverings may initially have been a reaction to the nylon shag-pile excesses of carpet manufacture, but it is, nevertheless, a product that is certain to endure.

Natural fibre floor coverings are hardwearing and cheap, though fitting costs are expensive as they need to be fitted by a professional, who will stretch and glue them in place to stabilize them.

Sisal fibre is extracted from the leaves of *Agave Sisalana* bushes, and is also used to make twines and ropes. As a floor covering, sisal is very hard-wearing and thus ideal for areas of heavy traffic. Seagrass is a patented floor covering with a natural stain resistance. Its texture is coarser and chunkier than that of other natural fibres, and it is more or less impermeable to water, making it ideal for rooms that are low traffic but where food and drink spills may occur. Coir is a hairy fibre, beaten from coconut husks soaked in water then woven either by hand or on looms to produce a floor covering. Jute has been imported from India since the 18th century and, in the 19th century, started to be woven for use as a carpet backing. It is the softest of the natural fibre floor coverings, making it an especially good choice for bedrooms.

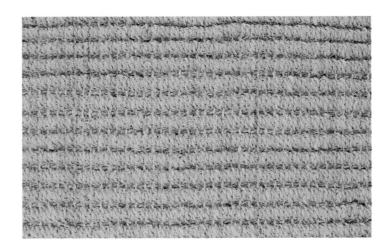

OPPOSITE ABOVE: Natural coir gives a handsome colonial feel to this bedroom. Its natural spicy hue provides a sympathetic background for the oriental rug, which provides a comfort for bare feet in the mornings.

OPPOSITE BELOW: Jute is less hard-wearing than other natural fibres, and so is not suitable for hallways and other high-traffic areas. It can be manufactured with a smart corded finish. Woven furniture continues the rustic aesthetic.

ABOVE RIGHT: When unbleached, coir fibres have a rich, gingery colour that instantly warms a room. For a wall-to-wall floor covering, coir matting pieces can be sewn together, and the edges finished with edging tape.

BELOW RIGHT: With its herringbone patterning and warm gingery colouring, this jute flooring makes a particularly comfortable and attractive floor covering. The softest of the natural fibres, jute is particularly suitable for use in bedrooms.

PATTERNS AND COLOUR PERMUTATIONS

Flat-woven natural fibres bring their own pattern to a floor. Jute, sea-grass and sisal are successfully woven into herringbone weaves with attractive chevrons. Diamond weaves and tight-fitting bouclés are also effective, while the simple plaited effect of a classic weave enables the fibre to be seen in all its raw beauty.

Different shades and permutations of the fibres are achieved through dying or bleaching. However, coir fibres, when bleached, can return to their natural, slightly ginger hue if they are exposed to sunlight. Similarly, natural fibre floorcoverings are mostly dyed with vegetable dyes that are not light-fast, so some fading of colour occurs through exposure to sunlight. This is intensified by glass. Jute is particularly susceptible to fading from light exposure.

Solid colours are available – rich reds, blues, greens and earthy blues, as well as modern blacks and greys. Colour can also be introduced in the warp threads of the woven fibre, creating muted shades and introducing new pattern elements.

Most natural fibre floor coverings have a backing of latex, which helps to prevent dirt becoming trapped beneath the floor covering, and allows the floor to be easily maintained and kept dust-free simply by vacuuming.

Natural floor coverings can be damaged by excessive damp or water and, for this reason, they are not generally recommended for bathrooms or utility rooms, though they could be used in a bathroom if treated with respect. They are also susceptible to staining, but inhibitors are available that can be applied to the covering before fitting. In kitchens, it is best to use a natural fibre rug, as neither carpet nor natural fibre coverings will wear well beside sinks or cookers.

Stairs can be an unsuitable site for some natural fibre floorcoverings that cannot withstand the stress of traffic, but protective stair nosings help to remedy this problem. For the best durability, the warp threads should be laid parallel to the stair treads, while the weft threads should follow the line of traffic.

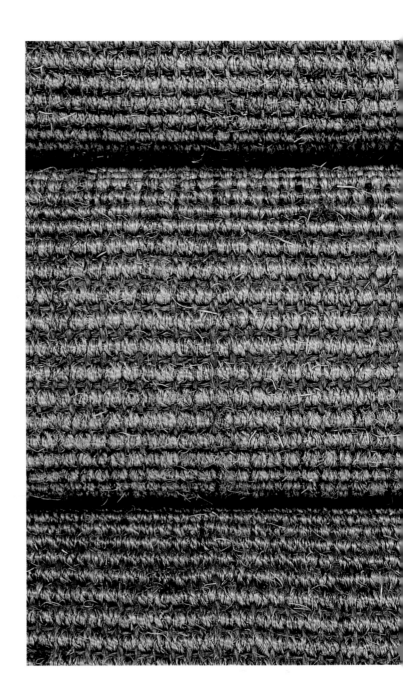

OPPOSITE: The introduction of differently coloured warp threads in these coverings serves to emphasize the texture of the bouclé weave of natural sisal fibres, as well as allowing the creation of a range of muted shades.

RIGHT: Denim-blue sisal flooring creates an informal mood in this bathroom, though natural fibre floor coverings such as this are not generally recommended for areas where they can be damaged by damp or water spillage.

BELOW: Loose, natural-fibre rugs are a good option for kitchens and other areas where a country feel is sought but fitted coverings are not appropriate. They should be kept away from areas vulnerable to water or food spillages.

TAPING A SISAL MAT

Natural floor coverings, such as coir, sisal and jute, are a popular choice for traditional and rustic living rooms, dining rooms, hallways and bedrooms. A small section of such matting also makes an attractive rug to add warmth, comfort and texture to a stone or wooden floor. Due to the nature of the fabric, it is recommended that the edges are taped to prevent fraying. Bound-edged rugs are commercially available but, if you bind your own, you can select plain or patterned edging tapes that will perfectly complement your colour scheme.

1 Measure and cut four lengths of decorative border tape to the same lengths as the proposed mat sides, then cut four lengths of binding, adding enough extra for mitring the corners. Lay the border tape face up on the mat just under half the width of the border tape away from the edge. Pin the border in place, keeping it parallel to the outside edge. Where the borders meet, cut the tape at a 45° angle, allowing extra to fold under to create a mitred corner.

2 Press the mitred corners then sew the border tapes in place, stitching along the inner edges and mitres only, with strong, carpet thread and an upholstery needle. Leave the outer edges unsewn. Position the binding tape face up around the edges of the mat, overlapping the inner edge of the binding tape over the outer edge of the border. Pin the binding tape in place. Cut the ends of the binding tape at a 45° angle, then tuck the raw edges under, aligning the mitres neatly.

3 Using a running stitch, stitch the binding tape in place along the inner edge to attach both the border and the binding tape to the mat. Leave the mitred corners unsewn. When all four lengths are sewn, turn the mat over. Bring over the free edges of the binding tape and pin these in place as before, mitring the corners. Sew the binding tape in place using hemming stitch, then sew the mitred corners on both sides, using small stitches and ensuring that the corners are neat.

CORK FLOORING

Cork is a material with many qualities that have earned its respect as a floor covering. This natural material is collected from beneath the outer bark of oak trees (grown mainly in Spain and Portugal) when it naturally sheds itself. Traditionally used for bottle stoppers, cork has been used more recently in a wide range of domestic applications, including wallpaper, wall tiles, and of course, floor tiles. Because of the way it is harvested, without the need for the trees to be cut down, cork is an environmentally friendly material from a sustainable source.

One of the best-known advantages of cork is that it offers excellent sound-proofing qualities. As it is also softer underfoot than other hard floor coverings, it is a functional alternative to strip wood flooring, for example, which can be noisy, especially in flats and apartments with neighbours living beneath.

Tiles are the most common form of cork flooring, and are usually available in a light brown or dark brown colour. They can be bought unfinished, in which case they will need to be sealed with coats

LEFT: Cork flooring can be painted, stencilled and stamped in the same way as a wooden floor. Here, the painted designs give cork tiles a stylish, contemporary look. Cork is an environmentally sound flooring choice, from a sustainable source.

OPPOSITE ABOVE RIGHT: A natural cork floor sets the same warm, natural mood in a home as a wooden floor, but it has the additional benefits of added insulation, sound-proofing qualities, and softness and warmth underfoot.

OPPOSITE BOTTOM LEFT: Cork flooring is now being produced by some manufacturers in a range of colours, from the jewel-bright ruby of this example, to more subtle shades. The tiles are designed to be glued to a solid, level sub-floor.

OPPOSITE BOTTOM RIGHT: Here a dark blue cork-tiled floor provides a sophisticated background to the citrus-yellow and pale turquoise-blue accessories in this interior. The colour of the tiles is intensified by their lacquered finish.

of varnish. Bought in this way, they can be laid in chequerboard pattern and decorated with paint, stencilling and stamps, much like a wooden floor, before varnishing. However, because cork is more flexible than wood, the paint will eventually start to crack. It is possible to lightly sand and reseal the cork, but this will only be possible once or twice, depending on the thickness of the tiles.

Smart cork strip flooring, manufactured as tongue-and-groove planks, is available, and it is also possible to buy cork veneer or solid cork, which is coated with a tough vinyl covering. Ranges include coloured cork, ranging from soft whites to blues and salmon-pinks, to co-ordinate with contemporary colour schemes.

Cork flooring is best laid with adhesive onto a plywood sub-floor screwed into concrete or nailed to existing floorboards. A cork floor should never be allowed to get overly wet or exposed to very humid environments, and care should be taken to stop water penetrating between the joints, which might damage the adhesive. The advantage of tiles is that if one is damaged, it can be replaced.

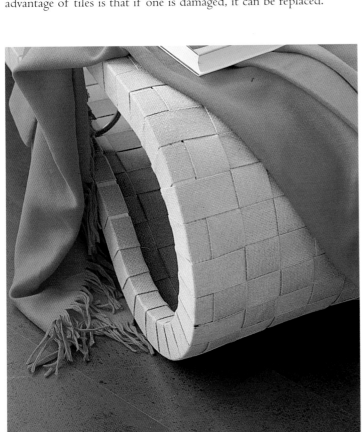

LEATHER, GLASS AND PAPER

Floors are now attracting more attention than ever before as a decorative surface – much like a fifth wall – and designers are searching for new mediums of decoration for them. As well as experimenting with pattern, form and texture in conventional floor coverings, inventiveness has brought new materials into play.

Using leather as a floor covering at first seems comparable to using silk as a wall covering – a lavish and beautiful concept, but somewhat delicate and impractical for domestic interiors. However,

leather is, in reality, no more impractical than the deliciously woolly and sensual sheepskin rugs that regularly appear in the cycle of interior style. As homes now enjoy a highly sophisticated level of comfort, warmth and hygiene, choice of flooring does not have to depend on purely functional considerations. A smooth leather floor will show scratches and scarring but this, in fact, will become part of its beauty. Leather can look particularly stunning as a central panel within a border of wooden flooring to take the initial stress of a room's traffic.

Glass is an adventurous choice of hard flooring. As the disciplines of the architect and interior designer begin to meld, futuristic materials can now find a home in domestic settings. Designers of urban habitats are experimenting with glass tiles, and even reinforced sheet-glass starts to open up the levels of our living environments.

Paper has made its appearance as a floor covering too — not in sheets, but tightly wound into a twine and flat woven with a linen warp to create a material that fits elegantly between the rough textured natural fibre floorings and woollen flat weaves. Traditional flat weaves (ingrain carpets), which showed an identical pattern on each side, have also made a reappearance recently, as have felted flatweaves, which are the closest to a fabric textile yet to be used as a floor covering.

OPPOSITE: Although the use of leather for flooring dates back to Italian Renaissance courts, its recent reappearance in interiors has been hailed as innovative. It provides a magnificently appropriate floor covering in this opulent interior.

RIGHT ABOVE: In sharp contrast to the rich, dark leather flooring shown opposite, this subtly luxurious, pale cream alternative adds a distinctly contemporary feel to the light-enhancing palette of creams and beige in this stylish interior.

RIGHT BELOW: Having grown accustomed to thinking of the garden as an 'outdoor room' where soft furnishings make their way outdoors, so gritty building materials are now bringing outdoor textures in to chic urban interiors.

INDUSTRIAL FLOORING

Despite its excellent qualities as a hard-wearing, serviceable material, rubber has never been considered as a domestic floor covering. Now, however, designers are attempting to put a bounce in our step, and are re-evaluating rubber as a desirable flooring materials for home use.

Rubber flooring is associated with industrial or commercial settings and, as such, has never been considered a thing of beauty, but rather as a necessary specification for factories, hospitals or public baths; but it is warm underfoot, with a safe purchase and a soft 'give' that makes it less tiring on legs than other hard floor surfaces. Rubber has now become available in a wide spectrum of candy-bright colours and patterns that are unmatched by any other flooring medium: bright marbled cerise-pinks, canary-yellows as well as uniform navy-blues make this material a major contender for modern design applications. Surface patterns are varied too: sheer rubber flooring gives a smooth finish, while raised dots and lines give the rubber a 'tread' for improved anti-slip properties, as well as adding textural interest. Like linoleum and vinyl, rubber can be cut to create imaginative designs.

Rubber flooring is best bought in tiles, which are easy to handle. A tile with a thickness of 2.5mm ($\frac{1}{8}$in) is perfect for most domestic applications, but tiles as thick as 5–6mm ($\frac{1}{4}$in) are available for heavy traffic areas. The tiles are laid on a latex screed to level either a concrete floor or a wooden floor reinforced with ply (marine ply for bathrooms and kitchens). Dedicated sealants are available and, once these have been applied, the floor can be vacuumed or swept then wiped with a neutral detergent solution for easy maintenance.

Following in the wake of rubber, other strictly industrial floor coverings are now being considered as flooring solutions by the avante garde and adventurous interior designer. Sheet zinc has appeared, creating a clanky, austere and post-modern mood. Steel flooring panels are also now being considered by designers, while the vinyl flooring company Amtico has produced a collection that imitates industrial panel flooring in lustrous metallic colours.

ABOVE: The watery sheen of a polished rubber floor reflects light in this modern office space. But even with an apparently shiny surface such as this, rubber flooring has inherent anti-slip properties that ensure safe purchase underfoot.

OPPOSITE: The raised surface of rubber tiles was first used in industrial spaces as an anti-slip device, but such patterning in rubber flooring has now become highly popular as a source of texture and interest for domestic flooring.

STAIR AND HALL RUNNERS

An elegant sweep of carpet can transform the most narrow, Gothic staircase into an inviting climb, but stair carpet undoubtedly receives the most wear of all flooring, as footfall is continually on just one area of each tread. For this reason, it is important to buy the best quality carpet or covering that budgets permit so that it will withstand the constant traffic. It is perfectly acceptable for stairs to be fitted with edge-to-edge carpet, but there is now a move towards the return of the traditional style of narrow carpeting, laid centrally on stair treads.

From the 1830s, when carpet first started to be made on steam-driven looms, it was manufactured in 70cm (28in) widths, which remained a standard for many years. As most stair treads were 90cm (35in) wide, a wooden border was left on either side of the carpet that had been laid over the stair treads. This is a feature that is still popular today, and most stair runners continue to be made in this width. The stair treads on either side of the carpet can either be sanded and varnished or painted in a complementary colour.

LEFT: The contrasting darker pin-dot pattern will help to disguise wear on this elegant stair carpet – a genuine boon, since this is the area that will receive the most traffic. The in-built border and traditional brass stair rods add a period touch.

OPPOSITE TOP LEFT: Modern designs for hall runners utilize the narrow specification of these carpets by creating patterns that enhance the natural boundaries. Wooden stair rods provide a simple finish for securing the carpet.

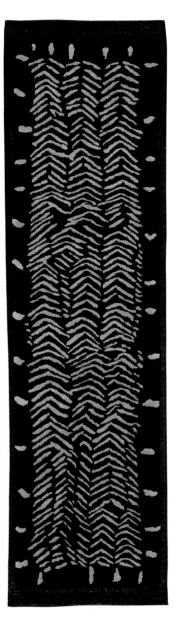

There are many stair runners available with border patterns, and these are usually integral to the carpet. However, it is possible to combine a main carpet design with separate border selections and to create a co-ordinating stair runner in this way.

In the past, when stair carpet was generally secured by removable stair rods, it was customary to buy an extra length of carpet so that the runner could be moved at intervals to shift the areas of wear. This technique helped considerably to extend the life of the stair runner. Although rarely used today, this is still good practice for a straight staircase without 'bullnoses' (curves around newel posts), and is certainly practicable with the new flat-weave stair runners available.

Just as traditional stair runners have integral borders on either side, so hall runners originally had borders woven into their design on all four sides. This practice had largely disappeared, but hall runners are once again being manufactured as a revived interest in traditional floor coverings creates the demand.

Hall runners are important for setting the mood in a home, instigating the transition from outdoors to indoors where comfort becomes paramount. Modern designs can add a twist to classic flagstones or wooden floors, and define a path into the inner rooms.

ABOVE: Pure wool flatweave carpets may feel much thinner than the woven tufted variety, but they do offer particularly good wear on stairs and are able to fit more closely to the treads. Abstract designs, such as these, make an unusual statement in passageways and corridors.

ORIENTAL CARPETS

When oriental carpets first arrived in Europe, they were so highly prized for their rich designs that they were considered too valuable to walk upon and displayed on the walls instead.

Carpet making in the Far East is an intrinsic part of life for those who make them. Indeed their lives are literally woven into the carpets, which are a vibrant and eloquent expression of the art, religion and history of the tribespeople and their villages, with all those elements woven into their carpets. For those people, the carpets are an important symbol of home, bringing warmth, colour and stability into even the most temporary homes for those who lead transitory lives, and thus embody the security of home.

Oriental carpets are the perfect foil for any style of interior. Equally at home alongside fine antiques or contemporary designs, their patterns and colours have a purity that renders them timeless. They are the most versatile of floor coverings and their designs complement every room, providing a welcome in the public area of the

hallway or luxurious warmth in the private domain of the bedroom.

Oriental carpets are made either of wool or, in the case of finer pieces, silk. Antique pieces are very valuable, but they can still be bought from professional dealers. However, oriental carpets are still being made today, using exactly the same techniques, which means that these beautiful objects, imbued with so much cultural symbolism and exotic cachet, are still available and affordable.

Oriental carpets can be laid on most floors. Plain fitted carpets, stripped or painted wooden floors, flagstones or sisal floor covering can all be beautifully offset with these richly woven pieces. Anticreep underlay is sometimes appropriate, and lightweight kelims should not be put over quarry tiles or flagstones, where they would quickly suffer wear from increased friction.

It is best to remove dust from oriental carpets with a brush sweeper. A vacuum cleaner is too harsh and will suck and wear at the fringe, which in fact consists of the ends of the warp threads, so great care must be taken not to damage these. Otherwise, the carpets are best beaten in the traditional way, and professionally cleaned by an expert once every five to ten years.

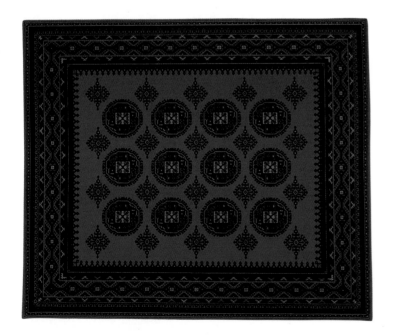

OPPOSITE: This richly patterned carpet contrasts well with the minimal lines of modern furniture, yet is muted enough to be in keeping with the gentle palette. The natural dyes used in old oriental carpets fade to an attractive softness.

ABOVE: A converted chapel is an appropriate setting for a faded wool rug, softening the clean lines of the modern alterations yet alluding to a more Gothic past. The tapestry furnishing accessories complete the look.

LEFT: Afghan rugs, such as this, are popular because of their rich, warm, red ground colour and the fact that they are hard-wearing and reasonably priced. The main motifs, known as *guls*, are interspersed with a smaller, stylized pattern.

KELIMS AND GABBEHS

Kelim is a Turkish word, meaning prayer-rug, and applies to rugs that are flat-woven rather than created by hand-knotting and cutting wool to create a pile, as is the case with other oriental carpets. In kelims, the threads forming the pattern are woven only where the pattern and colour make it necessary. Thus, in a kelim, the weft never goes right across the rug. The warp threads are practically invisible since the threads forming the pattern are beaten very close together. As a result of this method of weaving, there may be small gaps parallel to the warp-threads, where the different colours meet, unless the wefts are

hooked around one another or around adjacent warp-threads. Kelims are usually rather thin and soft, and are used in the East not as floor-carpets, but as wall-hangings and divan coverings. In contemporary interiors, a collection of kelims can really cocoon a room, creating the cosily exotic ambience of a tribesman's tent.

As they were used for prayer, kelims have a prayer arch incorporated into the pattern, which would be placed in the direction of Mecca when used for worship. Other common symbols may be identified, such as the garden, which represents the streams and paths of

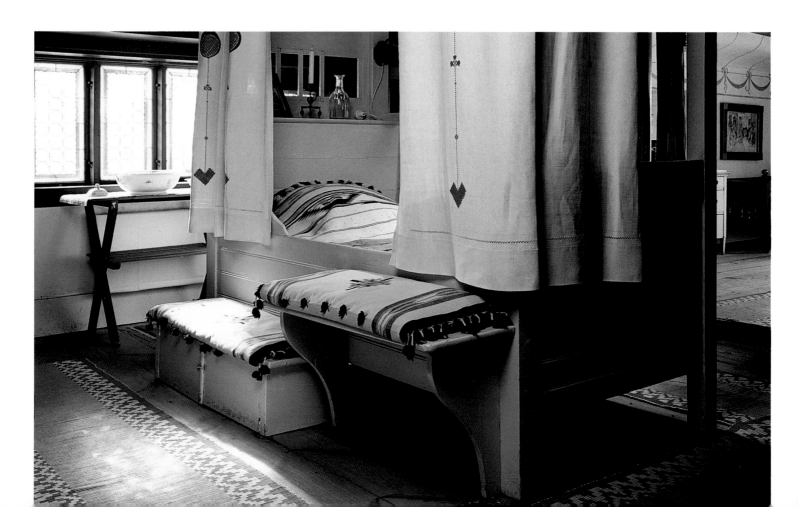

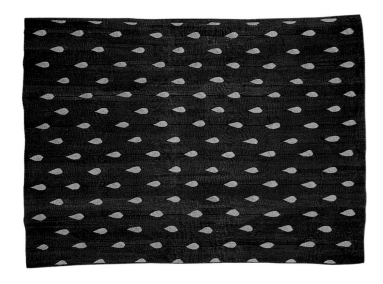

the classic garden, and the love birds, a symbol of life and freedom. Carpets incorporating geometric patterns are tribal pieces and make up the 'folk art' of oriental carpets; these are less formal than 'city' pieces, which are highly decorated with more fluid patterns.

Gabbehs are tribal pieces, too, made by Iranian nomads. They are woven with handspun wool and natural dyes and, as the weavers are given the freedom to be as creative and spontaneous as they like, no two gabbehs are alike. With their simple use of colour and naively woven characters and patterns, these rugs are particularly suitable for interiors with a light, contemporary mood.

To hang a rug on the wall without damaging it, construct a narrow, fabric sleeve on the back, just below the fringe, into which a bamboo rod can be inserted and suspended on hooks in the wall.

ABOVE: This simple, flat-woven rug has a powerful abstract design on a strong colour ground. The artlessly finished edges and glowing colours obtained from natural pigment dyes add to the earthy charm of the pattern.

RIGHT: A patchwork of tribal rugs creates an informal ambience in this sitting room. Patterns, colours and vintages can be mixed, much as they would be by the tribespeople who make them and pass them down through the family.

OPPOSITE: The lime-washed floorboards of this typical Scandinavian room are softened with traditionally patterned cotton woven runners in simple red and white, blue and white and green and white colourways.

AUBUSSON CARPETS

In competition with the exotic Turkish carpets that enjoyed such widespread popularity in the 19th century were fine flat-weave Aubusson carpets from the Creuse area of central France.

Aubusson carpets are beautifully woven carpets that have a enduring aesthetic. Much like oriental carpets, the perfect tones of their natural dyes and pattern means that they are pieces that fit effortlessly into almost any interior. Such a rug would not even look out of place in a stark modern interior setting, adding instead a softness and a flourish of stylized naturalism. That said, Aubusson carpets do possess a gentle, feminine charm that makes them particularly suitable for a serene interior. The traditionalist will find them the perfect adjunct to antiques and collectables, to fine ornamented furniture and to classic salon pieces.

Aubusson carpets originated from an atelier in Beauvais, in

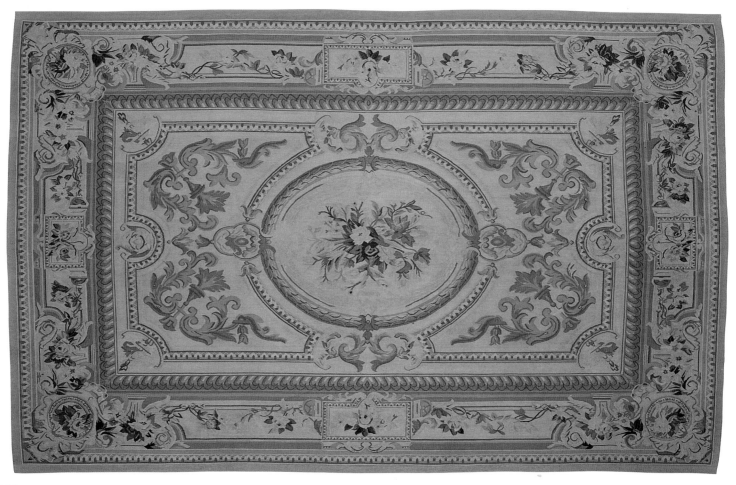

OPPOSITE: A traditional Aubusson carpet is a prized possession that could equally well be displayed on a wall or floor. The soft, muted colours of these carpets add distinction to a room, with their suggestion of faded grandeur.

LEFT: Layering richly patterned tapestry carpets over plain coloured fitted carpets adds a country cosiness and a touch of classic 'chintz' styling to a room that could otherwise seem rather formal. Tapestry-covered cushions add to the effect.

BELOW LEFT: In traditional, rich colourways of green and gold, this rug has a lavishly patterned, wide border, with a diamond-shaped central design. Fine rugs such as these are still manufactured today at affordable prices.

France, and were made for the chateaux and royal palaces of the 18th century. The fine flat weave of the carpets gives them the appearance of delicate needlepoint and, like any antique, original pieces remain extremely valuable. However, the patterns are well documented and exquisite Aubusson-style carpets are still being made today at affordable prices that match those of any other carpet on the market.

Needlepoint carpets, too, depict mainly stylized floral or naturalistic patterns and they are equally suitable for country-house interiors. Such designs are now produced in China and, like Aubusson carpets, make an affordable decorative rug that will help create an opulent impression of tradition and elegance.

A word of warning: it is often the case that these tapestry carpets are finished with a backing simply in order to cover up the threads left by the needlepoint embroidery, which can look unsightly. These backings, however, can actually accelerate wear as they tend to create friction, rubbing the patterned surface against the cotton backing. It is a much better to simply leave the back exposed: needlepoint was never designed to be reversible.

CONTEMPORARY RUGS

It may come as a surprise to discover that some of the most influential architects of the 20th Century have concerned themselves with carpet design. Frank Lloyd Wright, William Morris and CF Voysey all produced contemporary rugs at some point in their careers. Yet, for a long time, designers tended to associate fine carpets with antique oriental pieces and European designs, and therefore disregarded the medium as an outlet for creativity.

It was after the Arts and Crafts movement at the end of the 19th century that artists began to view rug design as an alternative medium. The Bauhaus movement embraced the Arts and Crafts ideals of the importance of craftsmanship, but extended them to include the new age of mechanical production processes. Both Gunta Stötzl, the female head of the Weaving department where most of the women who studied at the Bauhaus were based, and the Swiss artist Paul Klee (who also taught at the Bauhaus during the 1920s) created contemporary rug designs that are filled with stunning hues and geometrical or abstract shapes.

This sea-change in rug design had its beginnings not only in Europe but also across the Atlantic in America, where Frank Lloyd Wright was working his magic on the design cognoscenti with his innovative 'organic' architecture. His view that the furnishings inside the houses he'd created were intrinsic to the completed design meant that he too turned his hand to designing contemporary rugs that would sit well within his buildings.

Rugs only started to be of interest to a younger generation of designers in the 1960s, when the tribal rugs of Turkey first arrived in

LEFT: Bold, colourful abstract design makes the contemporary rug a work of art to be displayed in the living gallery of the home, adding textural softness to hard architectural spaces, as well as a distinctive statement of personal style.

OPPOSITE LEFT: Blocks of vivid blue and grey are held within a grey frame, making this modern rug a powerful focal point for a restful contemporary room. The blue of the rug is echoed in accessories throughout the room.

OPPOSITE RIGHT: Folk motifs, similar to those found on traditional tribal rugs, reappear in this bright and graphic contemporary tufted carpet. The cheerful colours and naive designs would make it ideal for a children's room.

Europe and America, the designs suiting the new spirit of the age. The newly-developed synthetics that had been initiated in the 1950s were now available for use, and the designers and manufacturers of tufted rugs began to find these nylon yarns attractive. The main reason for this was their low price when compared to wools and silks. After the austere designs of the post war years, the new geometrics and bolder colours that had begun to find favour with all soft furnishing designers were welcomed with huge relief by the shopping public. In contrast to the concurrently popular 'English Country House' look, these contemporary pieces were accessible and appreciated by all levels of society.

Even so, the majority of attempts at producing contemporary pieces remained on a large mass-production scale, and untufted rugs were not of good enough quality to carry off strong designs.

Today, however, covetable contemporary rugs and carpets are once again being produced by artists and designers. As our obsession with having wall-to-wall fitted carpet declines in favour of hard floorings such as wood and stone, a fitting decorative expression is required to keep pace with rigours of such fine materials. Stemming from the

BELOW: Natural flooring addicts will find that owning a contemporary rug injects a fantastic dash of colour, perfectly enhancing the golden tones of sisal and jute. Younger family members will especially appreciate modern designs.

ABOVE Abstract patterns are now widely available, carrying influences from leading modern art schools. These rugs add bright, bold colour to structuarlly plain areas, and can be used as a centrepiece in any room.

continental European tradition of laying these beautiful, natural materials on internal floors, we now seek rugs to decorate and soften, whilst simultaneously adding to the overall look of the completed room.

Hand-tufted pure wool rugs with contemporary designs bring the comfort required into the home without compromising the sharper, forward looking shifts in interior design. Urban fashion has its part to play in the increased interest and popularity in contemporary design. Over the past two decades we have seen an echo in London of New York City's craze for living in vast open-plan lofts. These bare-floored spaces are the perfect resting place for large contemporary rugs, and the apartments are in the hands of bright young owners who strive forcefully to create a home that is distinct and different from the living spaces that have gone before – fitted carpet is not an option. Their minimal interiors need textural softening in the form of underfoot furnishings that are equally cutting edge in their patterns.

However, there's no need to live in a converted warehouse to own a contemporary rug. Nor is living in a period property reason for only choosing a traditional Persian design to enliven a drawing room. Produced in a wide-ranging selection of designs that encompass bold and startling to neutral and retiring, contemporary rugs work just as well when placed in a room filled with antiques as they do when laid close to ultra-modern furniture. Owners will find that including a contemporary rug is a successful way to introduce modern patterns to a period room.

When choosing a contemporary rug, it is always best to think big – even in small rooms. Large floor canvases are suited to living areas, where they can be appreciated by all who walk across them. If you would rather start off small, opt for a design that will suit a bedroom – it's also less likely to be seen by anyone other than yourself. Natural flooring addicts will find that a contemporary rug injects a fantastic dash of colour that enhances the golden tones of sisal and jute. In modern living rooms, glass occasional tables allow the design to be uninterrupted by furniture. Younger family members will especially appreciate modern designs in dens and playrooms.

With designers such as Jasper Morrison dipping into rug design (see his 'Rug of Many Bosoms', 1985), and high street stores manufacturing their own striking ranges, the future of contemporary rugs looks certain. Now, British designers are asking the Oriental world to work for them, producing rugs in minimalist designs with a fresh and innovative palette of colours. Handwoven and using traditional skills, this new era of rug-making has done much to preserve the manufacture of carefully made hand-knotted carpets.

Canny individuals recognise that owning a contemporary rug can be a way of collecting an artist's work. The successful search for the ideal rug centres on finding one with a design and colour choice that not only appeals to you but also works perfectly when installed at home.

RUSTIC RUGS

In the 19th century, soft floor coverings became desirable for every room of the home, in both well-to-do and modest households. If a wool carpet was owned, this was kept for the best room, while simple home-made rugs were created for other rooms; or, if they were examples of finer craftsmanship, these were displayed in best rooms too.

One of the most charming type of home-made rug is the rag rug. Remnants of fabric or spare pieces from worn-out clothing or linen were always saved by thrifty housewives; these were used to create, among other things, beautiful patchwork quilts that are today highly collectable and admired for their needlework skills. In much the same way, pieces of cloth were collected to make floor coverings.

ABOVE: Simple, plaited country rugs provide an easy way to soften terracotta-tiled kitchen floors and tiled bathrooms. Scattered around rooms, they work well as colourful floor throws, adding decorative pools of colour and pattern.

LEFT: A traditionally made rag-rug floor runner helps to blend the multicoloured theme of this comfortable living room, incorporating, as it does, the vivid primary colours that predominate in the adjacent cushioned sofa.

America and Canada are particularly well known for their rag rugs, where the craft was introduced by immigrants from Europe and elevated into something of an art form, with decorative patterns designed and created by proud housewives.

There were many different techniques used for making rag rugs and, in North America, some were even made commercially on looms. One of the simplest methods is the plaited or braided rag rug. These are made from strips of fabric a couple of inches wide. The long edges of the strip are folded into the centre and the strip then folded in half lengthwise. Three lengths of these strips are then plaited to make a strong fabric rope. The rope is coiled and sewn in place with strong carpet thread, with additional ropes being added until the required size of mat is achieved. Another common type of rag rug is the 'proggy' rug, or in America the 'hooky' rug, where strips of rag are drawn through a backing cloth with a hook, to create a pile.

Unlike quilts, few old rag rugs survive to buy as antiques, but they are simple to make and are still popular as simple rustic floor coverings. Providing a charming and historically appropriate way of bringing warmth and colour to a quarry tiled or flagstone floor, they are perfect for country houses, and look pretty too on wooden bedrooms floors or as a decorative mat for bathrooms.

Buying remnants of cotton fabrics and making a rag rug is a simple way to make a floor covering that ties in with your room scheme, as well as creating a family heirloom that can be passed down through the generations. For beginners, kits are available that supply all the materials required, with simple instructions. A rag rug technique can also be used for other types of soft furnishing – a large-enough piece, for example, will make a cosy fireside blanket, bedcover or even a throw for the garden or to roll up and take with you on picnics – a chic way to take your style on location.

LEFT: A country-style rag rug, created in a pleasing soft palette of colours, fits perfectly with the restful tones of this room's colour scheme, as well as adding a welcome touch of comfort when toes hit the floor in the morning.

BELOW: The soft cotton rags used to create these rugs make them useful accessories to have in a living room, where they can be employed as warming rugs on chilly evenings or as decorative throws over furniture or floors.

SOFT DYED RUG

Whilst rugs are readily available in a huge variety of colours and sizes, it can sometimes be difficult to find the exact shade required to suit a particular colour scheme. However, small cotton rugs are easy to dye at home using proprietary cold water dyes – and the result does not have to be a plain, solid colour. There are several easy-to-achieve effects, such as this soft dyed rug with bold coloured ends gently fading into a pale centre. This effect can be achieved in any colour, but darker tones give the best results as the fading is more prominent.

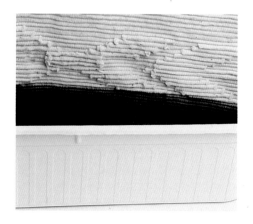  

1 Take a small cotton rug and machine wash it to remove any dressings. Mix up the cold water dye of the required colour in a trough (a plastic window box is ideal), following the manufacturer's instructions. Soak the rug in cold water then suspend it above the trough with just a small bottom section submerged in the dye. Leave the rug for approximately half an hour.

2 After half an hour, lift the rug out of the dye and wait until the excess water has stopped dripping out. Turn the rug the other way up and carefully suspend it over the trough, submerging the same amount of rug in the dye as was done at the other end. While the dye is taking on this section, the initial dyeing will begin to bleed down the rug, blending the colour towards the centre.

3 When the second end of the rug has been in the dye for half an hour, remove the rug from the tough, drain off the excess water and turn it upside down to allow the colour to bleed at this end. When the fading is equal at both ends, lay the rug on an old towel or a large sheet of cardboard and leave it to dry. Before using the rug, wash it according to instructions on the dye packet.

PAINTED FLOORCLOTHS

Rich wool carpets, rugs and fine woven tapestries have always been prized possessions. In the 18th century, Persian and oriental rugs were reserved for warming the floors of the finest rooms in the house – and then only in the most affluent of households. In cold kitchens and workrooms and, of course, in more modest homes, where one large room often served for dining, working and resting, something more serviceable was required to alleviate the unforgiving cold flagstones underfoot. The solution was the painted floorcloth – the forerunner of today's convenience floor coverings.

Painted floorcloths were part of the armory for creating a beautiful home with the most basic of materials. These floor coverings, which were both painted freehand and stencilled, soon came to be admired and treasured in their own right.

A painted floorcloth was made from sail canvas or heavy duck fabric, and was decorated by thrifty housekeepers or itinerant decorators, who derived their patterns from woven carpets, tiled floors and parquet designs. Once the floorcloth was painted, it was then sealed with many coats of varnish, and it is easy to imagine the similarities

ABOVE: Bold blocks of colour, framed by a Graeco-inspired key design in gold and ochre, bring a touch of ostentation to this relatively humble mode of floor covering. But in painted floorcloths, there is no premium on creativity.

LEFT: An appliquéd pattern gives a textural dimension to this contemporary floorcloth. This type of floor covering was at its most popular in the mid-19th century, but designs have always kept pace with changes in fashion.

between these early floorcloths and linoleum, with its jute or hessian backing and linseed-oil-based covering.

Floorcloths were particularly popular in the New World, where immigrants arriving in North America sought to keep pace with changing fashions with their painted canvases. It is there, too, that the craft survived the longest.

A renewed interest in folk art means that the quirky charm and serviceability of floorcloths are once again being admired and brought into service. While it is quite easy to make your own floor-cloth with today's fast-drying paints and varnishes, designers are also investigating this new medium, making and selling printed and sten-cilled examples. Sisal flooring, too, is painted or stencilled in situ with textile dyes for a modern take on this traditional technique.

Oil canvases are still supremely functional, their protective seal enabling them to withstand the traffic of footprints and paw prints in hallways, while preserving, undamaged, the pattern beneath, which can be as plain or as florid as personal preferences dictate.

These floor coverings are still ideal for kitchens, well able to repel debris, and are particularly suited to kitchen-cum-dining rooms where functionality must go hand-in-hand with comfort, informal family dining and providing a welcoming area for guests. There is something about their functional texture that also makes them mod-ern and relevant; laid across the starkest floor expanses in edgier industrial spaces, their workaday origins and simple designs make them practical coverings. On ubiquitous wooden flooring, too, they are a good-looking but pleasingly unostentatious option.

RIGHT: Traditionally, floorcloths were often stencilled with delicate motifs. Here, the simple ground of cobalt blue is adorned with white garlands and is evocative of classic Scandanavian style, in keeping with the innocent appeal of this charming children's bedroom.

MAKING A PAINTED FLOORCLOTH

A painted floorcloth makes an attractive covering for a wooden floor and offers softness underfoot as well as protection for the floor surface. Such a covering is surprisingly easy to make and geometric patterns, such as this bold, kelim-style design, are the most effective as well as being within the capability of most keen amateurs. The base canvas is marked into quarters, then the design is transferred to it from a paper template, applying the same template to the four quarters of the rug to create a pleasingly symmetrical arrangement.

1 Decide the dimensions of your intended floorcloth and draw a small sketch of the design on paper; runners and rectangular designs work best. Buy heavy-duty canvas, cut to size, from an art suppliers, adding an extra 8cm to any raw edges that will need turning under. Turn under the raw edges and secure them in place with iron-on hemming tape. Apply a thick layer of the base colour of matt vinyl emulsion with a roller; the paint will readily soak into the canvas. Allow the paint to dry thoroughly for two to three hours and then divide the canvas into four quarters, using a ruler and a soft lead pencil.

2 Take a sheet of graph paper the size of one quarter of the floorcloth, or join several smaller sheets to make this size. Draw one quarter of your design onto the paper, starting with a quarter of the central motif in the top right-hand corner. Bold, simple, geometric designs work best, and a border pattern adds a pleasing finish. Cut away the first part of the design, starting with the central motif. Lay the template onto the first quarter of the canvas and draw around the outline shape. Flip the paper and draw the same motif in each quarter of the canvas to complete the central rose.

3 Transfer the remaining pattern in the same way, cutting and outlining the outer shapes first and positioning the central patterns by eye. Paint the design, using matt vinyl emulsion in three or four colours. Use a small stiff paintbrush to outline each shape and a large brush to fill it in. The outlines do not have to be perfect; the weave of the canvas will give a soft line that adds to the woven look of the finished article. Paint all the shapes of one designated colour before moving on to the next. When the paint is thoroughly dry, seal the cloth with two coats of matt polyurethane varnish.

TROUBLESHOOTING

Floors need to be hard-wearing. The bedroom is the only room in the home in which the floor is spared heavy traffic. The best way to give your floor a long life is to provide a high quality sub-floor that is stable, level and solid, and importantly, if at ground level or below, to apply a complete damp-proof course.

Prevention is better than cure. Stain-resistant coatings can be applied to all fitted carpets, and with the application of one of the many available floor sealants and lacquers to other floor types, day-to-day care can be limited to vacuum cleaning. Every three to five years, most floors will require some form of maintenance. This will mean a professional shampoo for a carpet, a re-sanding and varnish of a wooden floor or a professional clean and seal for vinyl floors. There are, of course, remedies for dealing with problems as they occur. The number one rule with a spillage of any sort is to take immediate action. Use paper towels or cloths to soak up the liquid as soon as possible. This will make any subsequent stain-removal method easier.

LEFT: When laying a carpet, keep a good offcut for patching any burn or stain marks that may occur over the years. Look after your carpet by applying a stain-resistant coating and vacuum-cleaning regularly. Carpets should be treated to a professional shampoo every three to five years.

OPPOSITE: Prevention is better than cure; floor surfaces should be treated with one of the many available floor sealants and lacqueurs. The finish on your floor will partly determine the best method of care, so read any instructions carefully. Wooden floors will periodically require resanding and varnishing.

- A burn mark or stain that cannot be removed from carpet may be patched, so keep a good offcut when the carpet is laid. Mark a neat square exactly in between the pile of the carpet. Use a skewer in the centre of the square to lift the carpet away from the underlay and cut a cross in the centre to open up the square so you can push your hand through. This way the damaged square can be cut with a sharp craft knife without affecting the underlay. Use the burnt or stained piece as a template to cut your match on the offcut of carpet and fix the new piece in place with adhesive.

- Make patch repairs to soft vinyl sheet flooring in the same way as above, sticking the patch in place with flooring tape and using seam sealant around the edges.

- Carpet tiles are easily lifted and replaced in the same way as originals are laid, but when replacing other kinds of floor tiles, never lever them away from the edge as this will damage the neighbouring tile.

- Vinyl tiles that have been put in place with a latex glue may be lifted with heat, so cover the tile with aluminium foil and run over with a hot iron to soften the glue. Lift from the centre with a sharp implement.

- A broken ceramic floor tile or flag should be levered with a hammer. Chisel from the centre and always wear complete eye protection for this work.

- To remove burn marks from hard vinyl floors, rub them with fine wire wool until the brown burn fades.

- Fill pale scratches that show light by mixing melted candle wax with melted crayon wax to achieve the right shade, then using your finger to apply into the cleaned scratch to make a smooth and level surface.

INDEX

PICTURE CREDITS

The publishers wish to thank the following photographers, picture agencies and manufacturers who have supplied photographs for this book. Photographs have been credited by page number and position on the page: (T) top, (B) bottom, (L) left, (R) right, and combinations thereof. The following abbreviations have been used: Chrysalis Images: CI; Elizabeth Whiting Associates: EWA; Interior Archive: IA; Robert Harding Picture Library: RHPL; Sheila Fitzjones PR Consultancy: SFPRC

Page: 1 Brian North/RHPL; 2 Camera Press; 4 Camera Press; 5 Henry Wilson/IA; 6 Amtico; 7 The Merchant Tiler; 8 Alison Hopkinson; 10 Junckers/SFPRC; 11 CI; 12 Abode; 13L Mark Luscombe-White/RHPL; 13R Geoffrey Frosh/RHPL; 14 Abode; 15 Simon Upton/IA; 16All DIY Picture Library; 17 CI; 18 Alison Hopkinson; 19T Parker, Hobart and Associates; 19B Camron PR; 20 Alison Hopkinson; 21 Lassco Flooring; 22 EWA; 23L Geoff Long/Belle/Arcaid; 23R EWA; 28 Welbeck Golin/Harris Communications; 29 EWA; 30 Camera Press; 31 Camera Press; 32All CI; 33 CI; 34T Abode; 34B EWA; 35 Simon Brown/IA; 36 Bill Reavell/RHPL; 37T Bill Reavell/RHPL; 37B Tim Imrie/RHPL; 38All CI; 39 CI; 40 EWA; 41L Ken Kirkwood/Lyn le Grice/Arcaid; 41R Camera Press; 42All CI; 43 CI; 44 Paris Ceramics/SFPRC; 45 Fired Earth; 46 Classic Flagstones; 47L Stonell; 47R Paris Ceramics/SFPRC; 48 Stonell; 49L Fired Earth; 49R Fired Earth; 50 Paris Ceramics/SFPRC; 51L Stone Age; 51R Paris Ceramics/SFPRC; 52L Paris Ceramics/SFPRC; 52R Fired Earth; 53 Attica; 54 EWA; 55L EWA; 55R Fired Earth; 56 Schulenburg/IA; 57T EWA; 57B EWA; 58All CI; 59 CI; 60 The Scagliola Company; 61T The Scagliola Company; 61B Christopher Simon Sykes/IA; 62 Tim Beddow/IA; 63T Jakob Westberg/IA; 63B Tim Beddow/IA; 64 Paris Ceramics/SFPRC; 65L Simon Brown/IA; 65R Fired Earth; 66All H & R Johnson Tiles; 67T Andrew Wood/IA; 67B The Merchant Tiler; 68 The Life Enhancing Company; 69L Fired Earth; 69R The Life Enhancing Company; 70 Paris Ceramics/SFPRC; 71L Attica; 71R Rebecca Newnham Mosaics; 72All CI; 73 CI; 74All CI; 75 CI; 76 Tomkinson's Carpets; 77T Media Select First; 77B Media Select First; 78 Tomkinson's Carpets; 79L Stoddard Carpets; 79R Woodward Grosvenor; 80 Brinton's/Sylvia Herbert PR; 81T Camron PR; 82L Beeching, Dowell, Stubbs; 82R PGC; 83 Tomkinson's Carpets; 88L Amtico Image Library; 88R Chris Tipping; 90All CI; 91 CI; 92T Crucial Trading/Lara Grylls PR; 92B Beeching, Dowell, Stubbs; 93T Crucial Trading/Lara Grylls PR; 93B Crucial Trading/Lara Grylls PR; 95T Crucial Trading/Lara Grylls PR; 95B Nadia McKenzie/RHPL; 96All CI; 97 CI; 98 Black & White; 99T Simon Brown/IA; 99BL Camron PR; 99BR Camron PR; 100 Jonathan Pilkington/IA; 101B Henry Wilson/IA; 102 Richard Bryant/Arcaid; 103 Alberto Piovaro/Arcaid; 104 Brinton's/Sylvia Herbert PR; 105R Christopher Farr Handmade Rugs; 106 EWA; 107 Tim Beddow/IA; 108 Richard Bryant/Arcaid; 109T Christopher Farr Handmade Rugs; 109B Tim Beddow/IA; 111T EWA; 111B Sinclair Till; 112 Condor PR; 113L Simon Brown/IA; 113R Condor PR; 114L Christopher Farr Handmade Rugs; 114R Christopher Farr Handmade Rugs; 115 Andrew Wood/IA; 116T Condor PR; 116B Tim Beddow/IA; 117L Tim Beddow/IA; 117R Condor PR; 118All CI; 119 CI; 120L EWA; 120R EWA; 121 EWA; 122All CI; 123 CI